Autumn Romance

De-ann Black

Text copyright © 2024 by De-ann Black
Cover Design & Illustration © 2024 by De-ann Black

All rights reserved.
No part of this book may be used or reproduced in any manner whatsoever without the written consent of the author.

This is a work of fiction. Names, characters, places, and incidents are either products of the author's imagination or are used fictitiously. Any resemblance to actual persons, living or dead, businesses, companies, events, or locales is entirely coincidental.

Paperback edition published 2024

Autumn Romance

ISBN: 9798334018310

Autumn Romance is the fifth book in the Scottish Loch Romance series.

1. Sewing & Mending Cottage
2. Scottish Loch Summer Romance
3. Sweet Music
4. Knitting Bee
5. Autumn Romance

Also by De-ann Black (Romance, Action/Thrillers & Children's books). See her Amazon Author page or website for further details about her books, screenplays, illustrations and artwork. www.De-annBlack.com

Romance:
Autumn Romance
Knitting & Starlight
Knitting Bee
The Sweetest Waltz
Sweet Music
Love & Lyrics
Christmas Weddings
Fairytale Christmas on the Island
The Cure for Love at Christmas
Vintage Dress Shop on the Island
Scottish Island Fairytale Castle
Scottish Loch Summer Romance
Scottish Island Knitting Bee
Sewing & Mending Cottage
Knitting Shop by the Sea
Colouring Book Cottage
Knitting Cottage
Oops! I'm the Paparazzi, Again
The Bitch-Proof Wedding
Embroidery Cottage
The Dressmaker's Cottage
The Sewing Shop
Heather Park
The Tea Shop by the Sea
The Bookshop by the Seaside
The Sewing Bee
The Quilting Bee
Snow Bells Wedding
Snow Bells Christmas
Summer Sewing Bee

The Chocolatier's Cottage
Christmas Cake Chateau
The Beemaster's Cottage
The Sewing Bee By The Sea
The Flower Hunter's Cottage
The Christmas Knitting Bee
The Sewing Bee & Afternoon Tea
Shed In The City
The Bakery By The Seaside
The Christmas Chocolatier
The Christmas Tea Shop & Bakery
The Bitch-Proof Suit

Action/Thrillers:
Knight in Miami.
Agency Agenda.
Love Him Forever.
Someone Worse.
Electric Shadows.
The Strife of Riley.
Shadows of Murder.

Colouring books:
Summer Nature. Flower Nature. Summer Garden. Spring Garden. Autumn Garden. Sea Dream. Festive Christmas. Christmas Garden. Flower Bee. Wild Garden. Flower Hunter. Stargazer Space. Christmas Theme. Faerie Garden Spring. Scottish Garden Seasons. Bee Garden.

Embroidery books:
Floral Garden Embroidery Patterns
Floral Spring Embroidery Patterns
Christmas & Winter Embroidery Patterns
Floral Nature Embroidery Designs
Scottish Garden Embroidery Designs

Contents

Chapter One	1
Chapter Two	18
Chapter Three	33
Chapter Four	48
Chapter Five	61
Chapter Six	77
Chapter Seven	89
Chapter Eight	102
Chapter Nine	115
Chapter Ten	131
Chapter Eleven	148
Chapter Twelve	160
Chapter Thirteen	175
Chapter Fourteen	189
Chapter Fifteen	209
Chapter Sixteen	230
About De-ann Black	249

CHAPTER ONE

'I've never seen him before,' Aileen remarked, seeing the tall, handsome man stride across the village main street in the warm autumn sunlight. In his early thirties, his dark hair was stylishly cut to suit his classic features, and he wore smart casual clothes that emphasised his lean, fit build. Intense blue eyes surveyed his surroundings, unaware he was being watched from the front window of the bakery shop.

Set in the Scottish Highlands, near a beautiful loch, the village's main street had a pretty selection of shops, including Bradoch's bakery.

Penny looked out the window of the bakery where she was sitting with Aileen and Etta. The three local crafting bee ladies sat at their favourite table having afternoon tea and discussing the forthcoming autumn craft fair.

The annual fair was being held in the grounds of the nearby castle, owned by Gaven, the laird. The local crafting bee nights were held weekly in the castle's function room. The bee members often held extra get together craft evenings at their houses as well as attending the bee nights at the castle.

Aileen and Penny were in their thirties. Aileen had dark brown hair swept up at the sides with clasps emphasising her porcelain complexion and hazel eyes. She owned the quilt shop in the main street and sold bundles of fabric and thread as well as beautiful quilts. She'd pinned a notice on her shop door informing customers that she would be back soon.

Penny, an expert at sewing and mending, sold pre–loved garments she repaired and re–designed from her website. They both intended having stalls at the fair, as did Etta.

Etta peered at the man as he approached the bakery. 'I think he's coming in here.' She was in her fifties with silvery blonde hair. A key member of the crafting bee, she worked from home in her cottage by the loch, and sold her knitting mainly online.

'Do you know anything about him?' Aileen called over to Bradoch.

Bradoch, a fine looking man in his mid thirties, with dark hair and dark blue eyes, wearing his bakers whites, was behind the counter serving a customer, and bagging a fresh loaf of his popular oatmeal bread. His bakery had a handful of tables at the front of the shop where he served up tea and tasty treats for customers.

'No,' said Bradoch, glancing out the window at the man. 'He must be new to the village.' Bradoch's shop was the only bakery in the main street. And a hive of gossip and chit–chat.

Knightly approached the two–storey bakery. It had a modern vintage look to it and hanging baskets with autumn flowers in full bloom.

He pushed the door open and walked in. The bakery smelled of fresh baked bread, cakes and scones. The light cream decor and old–fashioned glass lamps created a welcoming glow.

The fire was set, but not lit on this warm afternoon. Spotlights illuminated the display cabinets filled with delicious cakes, scones, apple pies and other patisserie specials. Bradoch's royal icing skills were evident on the birthday cake and anniversary cake on show.

Heart–shaped iced biscuits were piped to perfection for those in the mood for romance. And lately, the village had been enjoying a few couples falling in love. Romance was certainly in the air throughout the spring and summer and showed no signs of cooling down now that autumn was here. No romance for Bradoch, but he lived in hope that one day the woman for him would waltz into his bakery.

Knightly scanned the array of cakes and scones, undecided from the excellent choices.

'What can I get for you?' Bradoch said to him, smiling pleasantly.

Knightly wasn't sure. He glanced at a vacant table for two.

Bradoch gestured to him. 'Take a seat. Would you like afternoon tea? I have a new menu for the autumn, including dark chocolate cupcakes and marzipan fondants.'

A sample of the delights included were displayed on a silver cake stand on the counter. One tier had sandwiches that tempted his taste buds, though the savoury pastries, scones and cakes on the other tiers were enticing too.

'Yes, that looks delicious.' He went over to sit down while Bradoch rustled up an afternoon tea.

Bradoch had seen him eyeing the sandwiches and added an extra two cheese, pickle and salad sandwiches to the cake stand. The honey pickle enhanced the flavour of the Scottish cheddar cheese. Jars of locally produced honey by the village's beemasters, father and son, Sean and Campbell, were on display beside a classic carrot cake topped with cream cheese frosting and decorated with little fondant bumblebees.

Jessy came hurrying into the bakery. 'Sorry I'm late,' she said to Etta and the others, and sat down at their table. She swept away the stray strands of brown hair from her otherwise tidy bun. 'I had to help Gaven with the guests.' Jessy, fit and in her fifties, had worked for years at the castle, and the laird relied on her to help with the smooth running of the castle's hotel facilities including the luxury cabins set in the magnificent castle's estate. In such a flurry, she hadn't noticed the man taking a seat at a table. 'It's been all go today with folk booking stalls for the fair. And Gaven's been busy talking to Struan on the phone about ideas to promote the castle and Struan's Christmas Cake Chateau.' Struan owned the chateau, a hotel further north in Scotland, and had been friends with Gaven for years.

And then Jessy saw the surreptitious looks the ladies were giving her, indicating the handsome man sitting nearby.

Unlike them, Jessy recognised him immediately. 'That's Knightly,' she whispered, but not quietly enough.

Intense blue eyes glanced over at the ladies then looked away. He was used to being recognised, and pretended he hadn't overheard them, feigning interest in the menu. Though he recognised one of the ladies.

Jessy had booked him into the castle the previous night and shown him to one of the luxury cabins where he was taking a creative break. The next day, he'd wandered down to the loch to explore the area and ended up in the main street which was only a couple of minutes walk from the beautiful loch.

He'd skipped breakfast and lunch, too busy with unpacking and settling into the luxury cabin. But now the hunger pangs were reminding him he needed to have something to eat. Seeing the bakery was ideal.

Knowing they'd been caught talking about him, Jessy made a fuss about telling them some other news.

'My niece, Amy, is staying with me. She arrived yesterday. She lives in one of the towns near here where she has her embroidery business. But it's handier to stay at my wee cottage to get ready to take part in the craft fair.' Jessy's cottage was situated near the castle within the estate. She lived alone and was happy to welcome her niece. Amy hadn't been to the village, but Jessy sometimes visited her in the town.

'I've seen her lovely embroidery patterns on her website,' said Penny. 'And I bought thread from her recently. She has a nice range of colours in stock. I go through a lot of embroidery thread for my mending.'

'I must have a peek at her website,' said Aileen.

'She uses her full name, Amethyst,' Jessy explained. 'But she prefers to be called Amy. She was born with the most beautiful amethyst eyes. It suits her perfectly.'

Jessy then saw her niece hurry past the window, all smiles and waving in at them.

Amy, thirty, had dark, shoulder–length hair, a lovely pale complexion, and wore purple velvet slim–

fitting trousers and a light violet jumper that suited her petite figure. She hurried in.

'I got caught up talking to Sylvie and Muira at the sweet shop,' Amy told them, planning to sit down, but all four chairs were taken.

Glancing around, she noticed the spare chair at Knightly's table.

Bradoch carried over the afternoon tea for Knightly as Amy approached.

'Is this seat taken?' she said politely.

Knightly had been watching Bradoch deftly balancing a tray with the cake stand and a teapot. He looked up to see Amy's beautiful lilac eyes, framed with dark lashes, gazing down at him. His heart took a jolt seeing the lovely young woman.

'No, it's not.' Knightly stood up before Amy could grab the chair and lifted it over to their table, sussing out the situation.

Three words he'd said, and yet the rich, deep tone of his voice sent a reaction through Amy.

Bradoch set the tray down on the table for two and wondered what would now unfold.

'Oh, thank you,' said Amy, letting him carry it for her. His tall figure towered over her.

At that moment, Aileen glanced out the window at her quilt shop across the street. 'I'd better run. I've got a customer outside my shop.' She got up and hurried away, leaving her chair vacant.

Bradoch watched as Knightly paused, wondering whether or not to take the spare chair back to his own table.

'Hello, Jessy,' Knightly said, filling the void of any awkwardness. And startling Jessy. He'd remembered her name!

'Hello, Knightly,' Jessy responded in kind. 'How are you settling in to your cabin at the castle?'

'It's lovely,' he said. 'Nice and quiet, luxurious, and the setting within the castle's estate is perfect.' His voice had a rich quality and a dramatic tone.

Etta was eyeing Jessy, encouraging her to invite Knightly to sit down.

Jessy got the message. 'Would you like to join us? We're just having a cuppa and a scone.'

He noticed they weren't having anything lavish. Tea and buttered scones with jam.

Four eager faces encouraged him to say yes, so he sat down on the chair he'd brought with him. Everyone made room around the table for the handsome plus one.

Amy filled Aileen's seat, and for a moment there was a lull as if he wasn't the only one thinking how had he managed to end up having tea with these ladies.

Bradoch brought Knightly's order over and sat the tea and cake stand on the table.

'Will that be all?' said Bradoch, sensing that Knightly couldn't tuck in to the feast by himself.

Knightly gestured to the cake stand. 'Could we have another one of these?'

'And another round of tea for the ladies?' Bradoch prompted him.

Knightly was glad of the prompt. 'Yes, afternoon tea all round.'

'That's generous of you,' said Etta.

The other ladies smiled at him.

'Are you all local residents?' Knightly's voice resonated in the bakery.

Etta made the introductions. 'Most of us. You know Jessy. She has a cottage on the castle's estate. I'm Etta. This is Penny. We have cottages by the loch. And this is Jessy's niece Amethyst. Sorry, Amy. She's from a wee town near us, and she's here for a short visit for the craft fair.'

Amethyst. The name matched those fabulous eyes of hers, he thought. Eyes that were viewing him with curiosity.

'Amy's staying with me to save driving back and forth to the town,' Jessy explained to him.

'I saw the poster in the castle's reception advertising the craft fair,' Knightly told them. The castle was used as a stylish hotel, and now the laird had added luxury cabins where guests could enjoy extended stays. The creative breaks at the cabins had become popular with artists, authors, musicians and others seeking somewhere to relax in beautiful surroundings.

'It's not a huge event,' Etta explained. 'But it's a big deal to us local crafters. Gaven, the laird, is generous enough to put events like this on at the castle.'

'We're all booking stalls at the fair,' said Penny.

'What type of crafts will be on display?' he said, encouraging them to explain about their crafts while he tucked in to the sandwiches.

He nodded, listening to them, taking in about their knitting, embroidery, quilting, dressmaking and making needle felted robins, something that Sylvia from the sweet shop had recently learned from Muira, her aunt.

'We must be overwhelming you with our chatter,' said Jessy.

'Not at all. I like to glean the nuances of people's characters,' he said.

Amy spoke up, having sat quietly sipping her tea and eating a chocolate éclair filled with fresh whipped cream. 'What is it you do?' she said to him.

'I'm an actor.'

Not even Jessy was aware of this. The booking from the previous evening hadn't given any details of his profession.

The smooth, gorgeous voice made sense now to Amy and the others.

None of them recognised him.

Another awkward moment was saved when Bradoch interrupted. 'Anyone want a chocolate truffle?'

These were added to the cake stands.

Taking it upon himself to explain his acting work, Knightly summarised his long and successful career. 'I'm a stage actor, and I've recently finished a summer season run of a drama in a theatre in Edinburgh.' He was well–known in theatrical circles, but those not acquainted with his stage work probably wouldn't have heard of him. He did receive coverage in entertainment features, but had concentrated on stage rather than film work.

'Is that why you're here, taking a creative break at the castle?' Amy said to him.

'Yes. I'd heard about the creative breaks at the castle on the radio,' said Knightly. 'A few acquaintances had mentioned the castle too, so I decided to relax and recharge here.'

'How long are you staying?' said Penny.

'I've booked a month's break. Then I'll consider my options. My stage work revolves around Edinburgh, especially during the forthcoming winter season.' Knightly shrugged. 'But considering it's not too far to travel from the village to Edinburgh, perhaps I'll extend my sojourn. I'm loving the relaxing atmosphere.' Then he looked at Amy. 'Is the nearby town you're from like this?'

Amy spoke up. 'The town is around four times the size of this village, and it's a lot closer to Edinburgh. It's easy for me to travel to the city when I need to, but I'm a small town person at heart.'

Knightly took this in. 'I've always lived in the city, especially due to my theatre work, but recently I've considered enjoying living in the countryside while being within a reasonable distance of Edinburgh.'

'My parents moved from the town to Edinburgh two years ago due to my dad's business. I live in a cosy little niche and visit them regularly. They'd happily welcome me to live with them in Edinburgh, but the town is picturesque and reminds me of the village,' Amy explained.

'But we're a hive of activities and social events,' said Etta.

Penny agreed. 'I moved here earlier this year from Glasgow to a cottage by the loch. I expected it to be so quiet, but Etta's right. There's always something exciting going on.'

'Like the craft fair,' Jessy chipped–in.

'I must pop along and see all the stalls,' said Knightly.

'Gaven has marquees put up in the grounds near the castle,' Jessy explained. 'The excitement is building already with lots of people booking their stalls and some crafters from further afield, like Elspeth, attending.'

Etta's face lit up with a smile. 'Is Elspeth coming over from the island?' Elspeth and her aunt, Morven, owned a lovely knitting shop on an island off the west coast of Scotland.

Jessy nodded firmly. 'Yes, Morven, is looking after the knitting shop while she's away. Elspeth is sailing over on the ferry for a long weekend. Bee has offered to let her stay at her cottage.'

Bee, Beitris, was an expert knitter. She'd recently moved from the island to the village and was staying in her aunt and uncle's cottage not far from the loch. Bee spun her own yarn and had supplied Elspeth's knitting shop, so they knew each other well.

'What about Kity?' Etta said to Jessy. Kity owned a knitting shop in a village on the west coast of Scotland.

Jessy smiled, pleased to tell her the news. 'Kity has booked a stall too.'

'Has she planned somewhere to stay while she's here?' said Etta.

'Not that I know of,' Jessy told her.

'Excuse me while I phone Kity.' Etta phoned her right away. 'I don't want her booking a bed and breakfast.'

'Hello, Etta.' Kity's smiling face peered out from the phone.

'Jessy says you're coming to the craft fair. You're welcome to stay with me at my cottage.'

Kity looked delighted. 'Are you sure? I don't want to put you to any bother as I know you'll be getting your stall ready for the fair.'

'I'd be happy to have you,' Etta told her.

'Thanks, Etta. I'm so looking forward to meeting everyone at the fair and seeing the castle.'

'You'll have a great time. Let me know when you're arriving.'

'I will. Thanks again, Etta,' said Kity.

'I hope Kity and Elspeth bring as much of their yarn as they can fit into their cars,' said Penny. 'I'll stock up on it. They've both got such nice taste in colours.'

The others agreed.

'I'm not a crafter like any of you,' said Knightly. 'But I can appreciate the work and skill that goes in to your crafts. I do love handmade items.'

'I'm sure you'll enjoy the fair, and have a wonderful time while you're here,' said Jessy. 'There are plenty of party nights and dancing at the castle, especially ceilidh nights.'

'I brought my kilt with me for such events,' he told them. 'The castle's website had video clips of the ceilidhs. They look like fun evenings, so maybe I'll see a few of you there.'

'You certainly will,' Etta assured him. 'Gaven invites the crafting bee ladies to all the castle's events.'

Knightly's eyes flicked a glance at Amy, picturing that he might dance with her, though he'd no plans to become romantically involved with any of the local ladies. Despite his reputation for being single and having dated a few actresses, he wasn't one for casual flings. And these past few years he'd felt a longing to find true love, the lasting kind, and settle down, or at least as settled as someone in his theatrical circumstances could manage.

'You must live an exciting life in the city,' Amy remarked.

'I do,' he admitted. 'So I'm keen to relax a little. Though perhaps I've picked a lively wee village to stay in.'

'Oh, you have,' Jessy said with a smile.

'But there's lovely countryside for walks,' Penny added. 'And the nearby cove on the shore for some fresh sea air.'

'I saw pictures of the white sand bay that's tucked into the coast,' he said. 'If I'd been here in the summer I'd have gone swimming, but I imagine it's a bit brisk now.'

'It is,' said Etta. 'But some folk still go in for a dook even in the colder months. We're fortunate with the weather here in the village. We're sheltered by the hills and trees. The summers are gorgeous and the springs and autumns are mild. Autumn this year has been warm and the forecast looks fine for the fair.'

'The stalls are all inside the marquees,' Jessy added. 'But we're hoping for a bright, sunny autumn fair.'

'When I was walking down the forest road from the castle, I could feel the warmth in the sun,' he said. 'The sunlight was glistening off the surface of the loch and I heard the bees buzzing around the flowers at the edges. There was a summery feel to it.'

'Our cottages have a view of the loch,' said Etta. 'Cottages are dotted around the loch and countryside.'

'I brought my hiking boots as well as my kilt,' he said. 'I'm planning to go exploring the whole area while I'm here. Nature's way of getting fit.'

'You look fit to me.' Amy's remark was out before she could consider it. 'What I mean is...you seem in great shape already. Fit and strong.' She started to blush, hearing herself sounding flustered.

Knightly's smile was warm and sensual, and the look he gave her made her blush even more. 'I'll take the compliment, Amy.'

Jessy checked the time. 'I'd better get back to help Gaven at the castle.'

Amy stood up. 'I'll head back too. Thanks for the afternoon tea,' she said to Knightly. 'It was nice meeting you.'

As all the ladies thanked him and got ready to leave, Knightly quickly settled the bill with Bradoch and hurried to catch up with them.

'Do you want a lift to your cottages?' Jessy said to Etta and Penny.

It was only a couple of minutes walk, but they took Jessy up on her offer and off they went, leaving Amy standing outside the bakery with Knightly.

Amy dug her car keys out of her bag. 'I'm parked along at the sweet shop, but if you want a lift back to the castle...'

Knightly smiled, nodded, and they started to walk along together in the late afternoon sunlight to the sweet shop. Reflected in a shop window, she saw how tall he was walking beside her.

He looked around him. 'It's a pretty main street.' He saw the wee shop selling groceries, the tiny post office, Aileen's quilt shop, a flower shop, and noticed the paintings in Oliver's art shop. Large floral watercolours were on display. 'Beautiful paintings.'

Amy glanced across at Oliver's shop. 'They are. Do you paint?'

'No, I wish I could draw or paint. What about you?'

'I design my own embroidery patterns — flowers, bees, butterflies, birds and seasonal designs. My autumn patterns are selling well, and customers are starting to buy Christmas designs.'

'So you're an artist too.' He sounded impressed.

'It's part of my work. I've always loved embroidering flowers and bumblebees and other little creatures.'

'I must have a look at your website.'

Amy laughed. 'I somehow don't see you taking up embroidery.'

'No, but I'm interested to see what you design.'

By now they were outside the sweet shop where her car was parked.

'Don't even think about looking in the sweet shop window,' Amy warned him. 'I was well warned, but couldn't resist having a peek.' She tapped her bag. 'Now I've got a selection of toffees and Scottish tablet that I hadn't intended buying. And two of Sylvia's special chocolate robins.'

'Too late, I looked,' he said, playing along. 'I saw all the jars of sweets in the window and feel the urge to buy a chocolate robin.'

'Avert your gaze,' she said with a sense of drama. 'Get in the car and I'll share my sweets with you.'

Laughing, he got into the car.

'Here's a chocolate robin,' she said, handing it to him, and popping a square of tablet into her mouth as she started up the car.

'You really know how to tempt a man like me,' he joked with her, taking a bite of the chocolate.

Amy nodded and mumbled with a mouthful of sweet tablet as she drove off. 'Don't say you haven't been warned.'

Sunlight was still glistening off the surface of the loch as they drove along. It was fringed with grass and flowers growing wild. Butterflies fluttered through the fronds. A scattering of cottages on the hillsides overlooked the loch.

'That must be Etta's cottage over there,' Amy told him, seeing Etta heading inside the traditional cottage that had a lovely garden.

Then Penny waved to them from outside her cottage as they drove by. They smiled and waved back to her. 'Penny is dating Neil the goldsmith. And Robin, a textile artist, is another member of the crafting bee. I haven't met Robin yet, but Jessy says she's now dating Oliver the artist.'

'Romance seems to flourish here,' he remarked, enjoying eating the delicious chocolate.

'Yes, so we'd better be careful we don't fall in love with someone local. I've been cheerfully warned about that too.'

'You're not dating anyone at the moment?' he dared to enquire.

'Nope. And not for a while. Romance and me...don't work out well. So I've been concentrating on building up my wee embroidery business.'

'Maybe you've just dated the wrong men,' he suggested.

'Oh, yes. I can pick ideal selections of embroidery threads, and design intricate patterns. But I always pick the wrong men to become involved with. It's not as if I go for bad boy types, troublemakers or anything like that,' she said, starting to reveal more than she'd planned. 'My last boyfriend was an accountant, but after a year, he decided to ditch me for the girl he'd really loved.'

Knightly felt the sting of that one for her. 'Then maybe you should try another tack. Date a less conventional man.' The urge to suggest someone like him took him aback. He managed to keep the comment to himself, but in his heart, he felt he wanted to protect Amy. The young woman with the beautiful amethyst eyes, and an open, trusting nature.

CHAPTER TWO

Neil the goldsmith made stealth moves along the main street, checking to see that his girlfriend, Penny, had left the bakery before he hurried over to talk to Bradoch. He wasn't the nervous type, usually, but he needed to chat to Bradoch in private about one of the most important things he'd ever planned to do.

A successful goldsmith, he made jewellery, mainly wedding and engagement rings, for well–heeled clients looking for something special, handcrafted to their specifications.

Wealthy himself, Neil was in his thirties, with light brown hair and pale aqua eyes. He had a penchant for classic clothes, bespoke suits, tailored shirts and ties. There was nothing outlandish about Neil. Obtusely, that made him stand out as being in a class of his own in the local village.

But this afternoon he just wanted to place a special order with Bradoch without Penny knowing what he was up to.

He was sure he'd seen Penny getting into Jessy's car, along with Etta. But as the group of ladies had left the bakery in a flurry of chatter, and some man, a rather dramatic looking person, appeared to be chatting them up, he needed to be certain that Penny wasn't in the bakery before he went in.

Bradoch was tidying up the cake stands behind the counter when he saw Neil's anxious face peering in the window. He sighed and smiled. It had been one of those days. Mind you, he thought, there were rarely any uneventful days in their lively wee village.

Neil saw that Bradoch had spotted him and, seeing that the bakery seemed to have quietened down after the busy afternoon teas, he went inside and walked up to the counter, glancing at the glass cabinet displaying the birthday and anniversary cakes.

'Everything okay, Neil?' Bradoch said to him.

'I was waiting until Penny and the other ladies had gone.' Neil glanced around. He was the only customer. 'I need to talk to you about something...secret.'

'I can keep a secret.' This wasn't entirely true, but he tried, most times, he really did.

'I'd like to order a cake from you.'

'What type of cake?' said Bradoch.

'Engagement,' Neil confided.

Bradoch smiled. 'Congratulations!'

'Penny hasn't said yes yet,' Neil was quick to tell him. 'And I haven't proposed. I'm planning to, once I have the cake.'

'When do you need it?'

'The day before the craft fair.' Neil didn't want to propose earlier than that as Penny was already busy planning her sewing and mending stall for the fair. And he wanted to avoid it clashing with either of their work schedules. They both had business meetings in Edinburgh on separate weeks. Waiting until later in the year would mean a winter engagement, or Christmas one, and Penny loved the autumn. He aimed to propose while the evenings were still warm, setting up his cottage garden near the loch with twinkle lights.

'I can easily do that for you, Neil. Did you have a design in mind for the cake? White royal icing? A chocolate cake? Traditional? Romantic?'

Neil's expression showed he needed Bradoch's advice. 'I've made the engagement ring, and I'd like to present it to her along with the cake. I'm planning to make dinner, then propose outside in the garden, having it all lit up with lights.'

'I'd suggest a classic vanilla sponge with jam and buttercream filling, white royal icing, fondant flowers...' Bradoch then had an idea. 'I have a folder in the kitchen with photos of wedding and celebration cakes I've made in the past.'

A customer came in and interrupted their discussion.

Bradoch beckoned Neil through to the kitchen and handed him the folder. 'Look through this and see if there's anything that takes your fancy.'

Leaving Neil to study the folder, Bradoch went back through to serve the customer.

Neil liked the look of a traditional, round, single tier cake with smooth, white icing and fancy white piping around the edges. Another cake had lovely fondant flower decorations. He thought a combination of the two would suit Penny.

After dealing with the customer, Bradoch came through to the kitchen.

Neil discussed what he liked.

'I can make that for you,' Bradoch assured him. 'I'll add pastel coloured flowers. And, if you want, I'll make a little fondant engagement ring to sit on top of it.'

Neil loved that idea. 'Yes, that sounds wonderful.'

'I'll create that in plenty of time for your proposal night.'

'Thanks, Bradoch. And I'd like to keep this a secret.'

'I won't tell anyone,' Bradoch promised.

Another customer had come into the shop while they were in the kitchen. When they went through to the front, there was Oliver peering in at the birthday and anniversary cakes on display.

Oliver was around the same age as Neil and Bradoch, tall, fit, fine featured, with dark brown hair, green eyes, and wore tidy casuals in muted tones. He sold watercolours, oils and acrylics of local landscapes and floral paintings, and lived above the art shop, having moved in the previous summer.

Originally working in the city, he'd found success there as a popular artist. But after taking a holiday, an artist's break at one of the castle's cabins, he liked the village and stayed to open his own shop. Since then, he'd fallen in love with Robin, and secured a publishing deal for the illustrated picture book he'd written. He was now working on his next two books that included his beautiful watercolour art.

Oliver jumped when he saw that Neil was with Bradoch. He'd hoped to talk to the baker in private, but later he had planned to chat to Neil too, so...

'Can I have a word with the two of you?' said Oliver.

Bradoch smiled. 'Yes.'

Neil nodded, wondering what Oliver wanted to talk about.

Oliver took a deep breath. 'I'm going to propose to Robin. I'd like an engagement cake. And an engagement ring.'

Bradoch pressed his lips together to prevent letting slip the secret, and glanced at Neil.

Neil blinked. 'That's great, Oliver, but when do you plan to propose? I have a few rings that might suit you, but I can design something to order, or alter the rings I have in stock.'

'Before the autumn craft fair,' said Oliver. 'I haven't got an exact date, but Robin is taking part in the fair with her textile art. I'd like to propose before the fair so she can wear the ring to the event. If she accepts.'

Bradoch and Neil exchanged a knowing look.

Neil nodded, giving Bradoch the go ahead to reveal his secret.

'I'm baking a cake for Neil's engagement to Penny. We were looking through the cake designs when you came in.'

Oliver laughed. 'We're both planning to propose?'

'This seemed like the perfect time,' said Neil.

Oliver agreed and told them his plan. 'I want to propose at night beside the loch. The evenings are still lovely and I think it would be romantic. Robin's cottage is at the loch, so I'm aiming to go for a moonlight stroll and ask her to marry me.'

Neil revealed his plan to Oliver.

'Your secret is safe with me,' Oliver told Neil.

'The two engagements are just between the three of us,' said Bradoch, and then beckoned Oliver through to the kitchen to select a cake.

Oliver had a heart–shaped, white–iced cake in mind. 'Robin loves flowers, so add fondant flowers. And could you write on it — *Will you marry me?*'

'Yes, I can write it in icing,' Bradoch offered. 'Do you want me to add Robin's name?'

Oliver nodded. 'Yes, perfect.' Then he smiled at Neil. 'What type of cake are you having?'

'A traditional round cake with white icing, flowers, and a little fondant engagement ring decoration.'

'Oh, nice,' said Oliver.

Another customer came into the bakery, Fyn, and Bradoch went through to serve him, leaving Oliver and Neil discussing engagement rings and cakes.

'What can I get for you, Fyn?' Bradoch said to the tall, blond florist, clad in a denim shirt and jeans, wondering if a third engagement was in the works. Fyn owned the flower shop in the main street and had recently started dating Aileen.

Although the romance was new, Fyn had liked Aileen for a while and they'd both flirted around each other, even dancing together a few times at the castle ceilidhs. Then Fyn had plucked up the confidence to invite Aileen to have dinner with him, and they'd quickly become a close couple.

'Two tattie scones and I'll have one of your cheese pastries,' said Fyn.

Bradoch smiled to himself. No third engagement today.

'I've been busy taking flower orders for the craft fair,' Fyn explained. 'I didn't have time for lunch, so this will keep me going until my dinner later tonight.'

Bradoch bagged the items.

Fyn paid for his order and then left with a cheery wave.

Oliver peeked through from the kitchen. 'Has Fyn gone?'

'Yes, you can come through now,' said Bradoch.

Finalising the cake plans, Neil and Oliver left the bakery shop and chatted outside, glancing to see if anyone was watching them.

'Come round to the cottage and I'll show you the engagement rings I have available,' said Neil.

Oliver hesitated. 'Can I pop over to my shop and grab a painting to take with me? If anyone sees me going to your cottage, they might suspect I'm ordering jewellery, a ring. But if they see a painting...'

Neil nodded. 'Great idea. There's always someone watching. It's hard to keep a secret in this village.'

Aileen was arranging pre–cut bundles of fabric in the window of her quilt shop and saw Oliver and Neil chatting outside Bradoch's bakery. Were they up to something? Then she watched as Oliver ran over to his art shop, and came out carrying a framed watercolour painting.

Oliver walked across to join Neil again and they headed away towards the loch. Neil must be buying one of Oliver's paintings, she thought, and then got on with sorting her display.

But she did wonder why they'd both come out of the bakery empty–handed. She'd seen her boyfriend, Fyn, pop in to buy whatever he had in the paper bag. His flower shop was just along the road from her quilt shop.

Shrugging off her doubts, Aileen busied herself with the quilt fabric bundles. She stocked a selection of quilting weight cotton fabric, other material, and sold the quilts she made. Two of her lovely new double–size quilts were on display. She planned to show them at the craft fair.

A pale golden sky arched over the loch as Neil and Oliver walked along chatting about the engagement rings Neil handcrafted. The day was closing down to make way for the early evening and there was a stillness to the surface of the loch.

Neil's lovely, whitewashed cottage was only a couple of minutes walk from the main street. They reached the front garden that was blooming with roses and other flowers, and bordered by a low fence that encapsulated the back garden too.

They continued their discussion inside the stylish cottage.

'I'm fortunate to know exactly what type of engagement rings Penny likes,' said Neil, leading him through to the back of the cottage where his workshop extended from a spare room. Light and airy, with a large window that let in daylight and offered a view of the lovely back garden, it was equipped with a traditional workbench and tables. Lamps lit the workbench area and cutting equipment. Shelves were stacked with boxes and glass jars of findings and bits and pieces for making rings, bracelets, necklaces and brooches.

Wedding, anniversary and engagement rings were Neil's top sellers. He had a small safe tucked under a bench where he kept valuable items including precious and semi–precious gemstones. And the gold he cut, filed and hammered to create beautiful rings. The rings, finished to perfection or being created, were stored in the safe.

Folders were filled with Neil's sketches of flowers that he often used for his ring designs. And like Bradoch's cakes, he had lots of photos of the rings he'd made.

'Take a peek,' he said, handing a folder of his latest designs to Oliver.

'Nice artwork, Neil.'

Neil smiled, taking the praise from a skilled artist like Oliver.

'Do you have any idea what type of engagement ring Robin would like?'

'I think she'd love a diamond solitaire.' Oliver remembered a comment she'd made about a friend's ring and noted what she'd said.

'A classic,' said Neil. 'White gold or yellow gold for the setting and band?'

'White. But I'm open to your advice.'

Neil showed him photos of this type of ring.

'Oh, yes, that's gorgeous. I can picture Robin wearing a ring like that. It's her style,' Oliver said, sounding enthusiastic.

'Couples often plan their engagement ring and wedding rings to team well, but I'll be able to design a wedding band for you if and when you want me to. Though you're under no obligation to have me design that too.'

'No, that would be great. I hadn't thought about this. I'm still wound up about the whole proposal,' Oliver admitted.

'So am I.'

'I don't know when to suggest a wedding date or anything like that,' Oliver added.

'From my experience, couples vary, so it'll be up to the two of you. But I plan to not let the wedding date drift. Personally, I'd marry Penny tomorrow, but...' Neil shrugged.

'I feel the same about Robin, but I want her to enjoy us being engaged and then plan the wedding date.'

Neil lifted out a box of engagement rings from the safe and put it down on the workbench under a light. Opening it, he took out three rings he'd been working on.

'This diamond has a scintillating cut.' Neil held the ring under the overhead lamp.

'It's like white fire,' Oliver said.

'The white gold setting enhances this particular stone. But here's another solitaire with yellow gold.' Neil showed him that ring too.

'They're both gorgeous, but I like the white gold and that diamond is a beauty.'

Neil lifted two pieces of gold from a tray and handed them to Oliver. 'This is yellow gold, and here's a piece of white gold so you can see the difference.'

Oliver was fascinated. 'Wow! This is the first time I've actually held pieces of gold like this.'

'They've both got their own special beauty and lustre,' said Neil.

'I can see why you love your goldsmith work.' Oliver held the gold pieces under the light. 'Though I can imagine the amount of work and skill it takes to create a ring from scratch.'

Neil smiled, and then showed him another ring, but Oliver liked the first one.

Deciding he wanted this ring to be finished and sized for Robin, Oliver felt relieved that the cake and the ring were planned. Now all he had to do was propose and hope Robin wanted to spend the rest of her life with him.

'Do you know Robin's ring size?' Neil doubted Oliver had this information, and was pleasantly surprised when he did.

Oliver dug out his wallet from his trouser pocket. Tucked inside was a fashion ring he'd seen Robin wearing, and he'd secretly borrowed it. 'Robin had this on the ring finger of her opposite hand, but I figured it would be close enough to the right size.'

Neil took the ring and placed in on the professional measurement equipment he had, calculating Robin's size.

'Fingers on the opposite hand aren't always the same size, but I'll work with this, make it marginally generous so she can definitely put the ring on. If it needs sizing, I'll sort that easily later on for you.'

Oliver liked that plan and shook Neil's hand firmly. 'You've been a terrific help.'

'Are you taking part in the craft fair? Showing your artwork?' Neil said, tidying away the rings again to keep them safe, planning to work on Robin's ring later.

Oliver shook his head. 'No, I'm going to be helping Robin with her textile art stall. Just being there to back her up if she needs anything. What about you? Are you showing your goldwork?'

'No, I'm the same as you. I've promised to help Penny with her sewing and mending stall. She's been organising some lovely vintage garments, like a denim jacket, that she's embroidered beautifully.'

'I'll propose to Robin two nights before the fair,' said Oliver, hearing that Neil planned his proposal one night prior to the event. He didn't want their special nights to clash.

'Okay, I'll work on the ring and have it ready in plenty of time for you,' Neil promised.

They were discussing what type of ring box to select when Penny came in all smiles, her blonde hair tied back in a ponytail, eager to chat to Neil. She was surprised and pleased to see Oliver.

'What are you two up to?' Penny said. Her lovely pale grey eyes looked curious.

Neil hesitated, but Oliver filled in with a plausible excuse. 'Neil wanted to borrow one of my paintings to use as a background for photos of his latest rings on his website.' He looked at Neil for back–up.

'Yes,' Neil agreed.

Oliver grabbed the painting where he'd left it and held it up.

'I love those watercolour flowers,' said Penny.

Neil smiled tightly.

Penny explained why she'd dropped by. 'Jessy phoned me. She's organised an impromptu get together at the castle this evening for the crafting bee ladies to discuss their plans for the fair. I'm going along.'

Neil smiled. 'Great idea. It'll let you finalise some of your plans for the stall.'

'Exactly, so I'll call you later,' said Penny, and then she happily headed away again.

'Phew!' Oliver sighed heavily. 'That was close. But I don't think she suspected what we're up to.'

'No, but I'll take a few photos of my new wedding ring designs with your painting just in case she tells Robin you were here.'

Oliver agreed.

Robin was working on an intricate piece of textile art in her cottage. The whitewashed cottage overlooked the loch and she had the window open to let the fresh air waft in.

She'd been working on it all day, adding pieces of chiffon and lace to the landscape she'd painted on to white cotton fabric. Now she was hand stitching the details with embroidery thread. It was almost finished, and it was a piece she planned to show at the fair.

Her phone rang and she checked the caller, thinking it would be Oliver phoning to ask if she wanted to have dinner with him. But it was Jessy.

'I'm organising a wee get together for the crafting bee ladies at the castle this evening to talk about our plans for our stalls at the fair,' said Jessy. 'Would you like to come along? I know it's short notice, but the function room is free this evening, and Gaven is happy to let us use it.'

'I'd be happy to go. I've been working all day on a new piece for my stall, and I'd like to chat about the plans for the fair.'

'Well, pop up and join us. I'm phoning all the ladies and my niece, Amy, will be there, so you'll meet her. She's staying with me at my cottage.'

'I'll have a quick dinner and then come up to the castle,' said Robin.

'No, Gaven's laying on a snack dinner for us. Chef's letting us try his new recipe lentil and vegetable soup. And we'll have tea and cake or a scone. Nothing fancy, but tasty.'

'Even better. I'll get tidied and drive up. Thanks, Jessy.'

'See you in a wee while.'

Robin left her piece of textile art to dry thoroughly, and got ready to go.

Apart from her textile art, Robin sometimes modelled knitwear. Her jeans suited her slender figure and she wore a pretty floral top. In her early thirties, she had porcelain skin, blue eyes, and long, strawberry–blonde hair.

She messaged Oliver about her evening with the crafting bee ladies, and then picking up her craft bag, she drove up the forest road to the castle.

The evergreens created a lush setting, mixed with the rich autumn colours of the other trees overarching the road. It was a scene she'd previously made as a textile art painting. Layering leaf greens to deepest emerald in paint and fabric texture, from smooth cotton to chiffon, she'd stitched it with embroidery thread and crewel wool. No wonder the castle's creative breaks were popular with all types of artists, she thought, for the local area's natural beauty continued to spark her imagination. She now wanted to work with these gorgeous colours to design another piece of textile art.

It was a fairly short drive from the loch to the castle's estate, and she kept the car windows open to breathe in the fresh, early evening air. The scent of the trees and greenery was refreshing and she was looking forward to chatting about the fair.

Robin was a recent addition to the community from the city, and this would be her first year at the craft fair. But she'd been looking at the pictures that Gaven had put up on the castle's website of previous years to promote the event.

There were plenty of activities and parties in the close–knit community, and her social life was busier than it had been when she lived in the city. But her work schedule was busy too, including a forthcoming trip to Edinburgh for work, and a knitwear photo–shoot soon. Then there was the local winter celebrations to look forward to, including a winter fair and the Christmas ball.

A busy time ahead. Robin smiled to herself. At least her life with Oliver was settled now that they were dating.

CHAPTER THREE

The magnificent castle was aglow in the mellow early evening sunlight. The remnants of the lovely autumn day were refusing to go quietly into the night. A sky of golden tones to warm pinks and lilac arched above the castle.

Set within the beautiful estate that bordered the forest, the castle had a fairytale quality with two turrets rising high above the main structure. Gaven lived in one of the turrets that had a view of the loch and surrounding countryside.

The luxury cabins were dotted amid the estate, within easy reach of the castle, but each tucked out of view, creating niches of privacy for the guests. Due to popularity, new cabins were being added.

Penny drove through the wide open ornate gates, admiring the extensive gardens and well–kept lawns, and up to the front entrance. The doors were open and the windows were glowing with lights, creating a welcoming atmosphere.

Robin had just arrived outside the castle, and when she saw Penny, she waited so they could walk in together.

'I brought my craft bag too,' Robin said, tapping her bag filled with a couple of items she could mend with her creative embroidery. 'I wasn't sure if we'd be doing any crafting or just chatting and making plans for the fair.'

Penny shrugged her craft bag up on to her shoulder as they walked up to the entrance. 'Neither did I, but I brought it along anyway.'

Gaven was standing behind the front desk with Walter as Penny and Robin walked into the reception. The castle's decor was a mix of traditional elements with touches of modern styling. As Penny and Robin walked across the plush tartan carpeting, they heard the sounds of chatter coming from the function room.

Gaven was talking on the phone again to Struan, about the castle and the Christmas Cake Chateau, and nodded acknowledgement to Penny and Robin as they arrived while continuing his conversation.

The laird was in his thirties and had rich auburn hair, grey–green eyes and a fit build. He kept himself fit by running around the loch in the evenings, and was considered to be a local heartthrob with a kind and generous heart. He was single, but like Bradoch, he hoped one day the woman for him would waltz into his life. Meantime, he put all his energy in to the running of the castle's hotel facilities and organising events for the local community and the guests.

Gaven was always well–dressed, and wore formal dark trousers, a white shirt, silk tie and a dark waistcoat. For the ceilidh nights, he wore his kilt.

Walter, a mature and cheery character, was the castle's handyman and a key member of staff, helping to deal with guests and general tasks.

'Jessy and the ladies are through in the function room,' Walter called over to Penny and Robin.

'Thanks, Walter,' said Robin.

Penny smiled over to Walter too.

And through they went to find several members of the crafting bee seated at tables chatting about the fair. Amy was there too, sitting near Sylvia and Muira from the sweet shop.

Knitting, sewing, quilting, dressmaking, crochet, needle felting, and all sorts of crafts were being discussed by the ladies.

Etta and Jessy were seated together and waved Penny and Robin over to their table to join them.

Jessy held up a photo album. 'This is the album from the past few fairs we've had at the castle. Take a peek. It has extra photos that aren't up on the website. You'll see the layout of the stalls. Gaven's planning to keep the two large marquees the same as before.'

Robin took the album from Jessy and started to look through the pictures, sharing it with Penny.

Etta spoke up. 'Bee phoned to say she'll be a wee bit late, but she'll be here. And Aileen is on her way too.'

Bee was busy finishing orders for a Fair Isle jumper and a lace weight chemise for her online customers.

Aileen had been finishing a quilt that was due to be picked up by a customer in the morning from her quilt shop.

Gaven came striding through to the function room to talk to the ladies. 'Chef's preparing dinner for the guests, and your meal will be served up in about half an hour.'

Chef and his staff worked in the castle's massive kitchen and it was always a well–organised hive of activity. The new menus for the autumn were still being updated. The cuisine was popular with guests. And those living locally were welcome to have lunch and dinner in the restaurant.

'Thank you, Gaven,' said Jessy.

'I was just speaking to Struan, and he's coming down from the Christmas Cake Chateau to attend the craft fair,' Gaven told them. Most of them knew about Struan. He was a long–time friend of the laird and lately they'd been helping each other to promote their respective hotel facilities.

'Elspeth has confirmed that she's coming over from the island,' Jessy told Gaven. 'And Kity from the knitting shop on the west coast is attending too. But they won't need accommodation because Etta and Bee are putting them up for the weekend.'

'That's handy,' said Gaven. 'The fair's bookings are really taking off, so we need every spare room and nook and cranny available.'

The castle was the only hotel in the village, but numerous cottages and farmhouses offered bed and breakfast accommodation whenever there was a local event.

As they were talking, an inquisitive face peered into the function room.

'Oh, there's Knightly,' Jessy exclaimed.

Gaven headed over to the actor. 'How are you liking your cabin?' he said, shaking hands with Knightly.

'It couldn't be better. My main problem is...I think I'm going to find it difficult to leave and go back home to Edinburgh when my stay is finished,' he said, smiling.

'Well, a few guests on our creative breaks have ended up moving to the village,' said Gaven. 'Including Neil the goldsmith, and our local artist, Oliver.'

'I've seen the wonderful paintings in Oliver's art shop,' said Knightly. He glanced at the ladies. 'Jessy kindly invited me to join her and the ladies for afternoon tea at Bradoch's bakery today. And thanks to Amy, I narrowly escaped disappearing into the temptations of the sweet shop.'

Gaven and the ladies laughed, and Jessy gestured to Sylvia and Muira, introducing them to Knightly.

'Delighted to meet you,' said Knightly in a voice that resonated in the function room. 'I thoroughly enjoyed the chocolate robin Amy gave me. Delicious chocolate.'

A blush formed on Sylvia's pale cheeks at the compliment. She was in her early thirties, with green eyes and shoulder–length blonde hair. She was currently dating Laurie, a well–known singer and musician. Laurie had come from Edinburgh to take a creative break at the castle and fallen in love with Sylvia.

Muira spoke up. 'My niece, Sylvia, is hoping to be a chocolatier one day, and she's created some tasty new sweets for the shop. Pop in and be tempted.'

'I shall.' Knightly's tone left them in no doubt that he would.

Muira, similar in age to Etta, was happy that Sylvia had moved to the village to work at her sweet shop.

'Do you want to join us?' Etta said to Knightly. 'We're chatting about the craft fair, but we're having a wee dinner soon. Unless you're dining through in the restaurant.'

Knightly was keen to take them up on their invitation. 'If you're sure I'm not interrupting your evening.'

'Come away in.' Etta waved him to come over and join them.

Gaven smiled at Knightly. 'I'll tell chef you're dining with the ladies.'

'I know I have self–catering facilities in my cabin,' said Knightly. 'But I'll probably have quite a few meals at the castle.'

'Yes, do that,' Gaven told him. 'Remember, breakfasts are served every morning in the guests' dining room, and talk to Walter about any groceries you'd like delivered to your cabin.'

'That's handy, I will,' said Knightly.

Heading away to tell chef about the added guest in the function room, Gaven left Knightly in the welcoming hands of the ladies.

The actor was seated in the hub of them, and introduced to everyone.

'Am I expected to knit or sew something to earn my supper?' Knightly joked with them.

The ladies laughed.

'Are you into any crafts yourself?' Sylvia said to him.

'Nooo, but I'm looking forward to browsing the stalls at the fair.'

'We're just discussing our plans for the fair,' Jessy told him. Then she showed the ladies the current plan for the stalls in one of the marquees.

This was eagerly passed around the ladies, and even Knightly had a peek at it.

'Most of the stalls have now been taken,' said Jessy. 'Those of you that attended the fairs before know roughly how the event goes. But as we've several newcomers this year, including Penny, Robin, Sylvia, Bee and Amy, I thought I'd give you a rundown of the schedule.'

This was discussed with interest, and Knightly joined in the chat.

Walter wheeled in a silver tea trolley with cups of tea, milk and sugar. 'Here's a cuppa to wet your whistles, while you chat, before you get your dinner.'

'Thank you, Walter,' said Jessy.

'Walter!' Knightly announced. 'I believe you're the man to talk to about having groceries delivered to my cabin.'

'I am indeed,' said Walter. 'Are you into cooking?'

'I can cook, but nothing too fancy,' Knightly explained. 'I used to cook more often, but nowadays with the theatre work, I dine in restaurants a lot, so I'm a bit out of practise with rustling up a dinner for myself.'

'I can give you a grocery list for you to tick what you like and don't like,' Walter offered.

'I'm not a fussy eater, Walter.'

'Well, how about I get a general grocery delivery for you. Fresh milk, bread, butter, Scottish cheddar, porridge and the like should be in your cabin fridge and cupboards already.'

'Yes, I've made myself tea so far.' Knightly smiled. 'Thankfully, I've wangled being invited to eat twice with the ladies. But I'm thinking that tomorrow I'll need to start fending for myself.'

'I'll sort your groceries out for you, Knightly,' Walter said chirpily, and off he went, letting them enjoy their tea and chatter.

'Remember, you can have your meals here in the castle,' Jessy reminded him. 'And it sounds like you're used to fine dining in city restaurants.'

'I am, Jessy.' Knightly's expression then took on a faraway look. 'But there's nothing like a home cooked dinner after a long day. I can't remember the last time I had that.' He invariably came home to a beautiful but empty house. 'It's been a while.'

A lull descended, with the ladies realising that for all his success, this man didn't have the warmth and comfort of the things in life most of them enjoyed all the time.

'I didn't mean to bring the mood down, ladies,' Knightly said, upping his tone. 'I'm happy with my lot.'

But Amy sensed the actor in him putting on a performance, not lying, but not revealing how much he missed a home cooked dinner. She felt the urge to offer to make him dinner one night at Jessy's cottage when her aunt was working in the hotel. But she held back, not wanting to seem like she was luring him into any awkward situation, especially as he could construe it having romantic overtures.

The mood lifted and the chatter turned back to crafting.

While they were talking, Aileen hurried in. 'Sorry I'm late, but I had a quilt to finish at the shop.' Then she noticed Knightly. 'Oh, hello again.'

Knightly smiled. 'Don't worry, Aileen, I'm not here to knit or sew. I've just somehow wangled my second invitation to join you ladies for something to eat. I seem to be making a habit of it.'

Aileen laughed.

Then Bee came hurrying in too. 'Have I missed anything?' She wondered about the man sitting in their midst, but made no comment. Fairly new to the village, she still didn't know everyone.

'No,' Etta assured her. 'We're just looking over the schedule.' She handed it to Bee. 'And this is Knightly. He's a successful stage actor on a break here from Edinburgh.'

'Nice to meet you,' said Bee.

'And you,' he said. 'Are you a quilter, dressmaker—'

'Knitter,' Bee cut–in.

'An expert knitter,' Etta told him. 'And Bee spins her own yarn.'

'There's so much more to everyone's crafting than I'd imagined,' he said, genuinely impressed.

'I've been learning other crafts,' Penny told him. 'Everyone shares their knowledge and expertise.'

'Muira taught me needle felting,' said Sylvia.

'I don't even know what that is,' Knightly confessed.

Sylvia dug out a couple of items from her bag. 'This is a needle felted robin I made. I've made three now. And I've started on an owl.' She handed them over to Knightly.

'Oh, I see, it's felted creatures,' he said, studying the robin and the makings of an owl. 'I've seen items like these for sale in craft shops. I never knew it was called needle felting.' He admired her handiwork. 'These are so cute. They must be fun to make too.' Then he handed them back.

'They are,' Sylvia agreed. 'I love quilting too, and Aileen had this amazing sweet print fabric that she used to make us aprons for the sweet shop. I'm making a quilt for my bed from the fabric as well.'

Sylvia looked up pictures on the shop's website of them wearing the aprons. She held her phone up to show Knightly.

The chatter continued, with Knightly learning more about the crafting bee, and the ladies making plans for the fair.

Then Jessy remembered something. 'Gaven wanted me to ask if any of you would be willing to give demonstrations of your crafts when you're at your stalls. We usually just display and sell our crafts. But Struan said he had a craft event at his chateau and the demonstrations were popular.'

'I'd be happy to demonstrate my knitting,' Bee offered. 'It'd be like the wee videos I put up on my website showing how I knit and spin the yarn.'

Etta spoke up. 'I could show how I knit cables on jumpers, or whatever else you think would be of interest.'

'I'll demonstrate my embroidery,' Amy added. 'I could show various stitching techniques with stranded cotton thread. And crewel work, embroidering with crewel wool.'

Jessy noted their names down so she could tell Gaven.

A sewing and mending demonstration was offered by Penny. 'I could show how to do invisible mending, and visible mending using bright coloured thread, and embroidery techniques to mend a tear or worn fabric on garments.'

Robin added her textile art techniques to the list.

Aileen offered to demonstrate quilting, how to make hexies for a patchwork quilt, and hand sew on binding.

Jessy wrote down Elspeth and Kity's names too. 'I'm sure they'll want to demonstrate their knitting. I'll phone them.'

All of the members present were willing to give demonstrations at their stalls.

Jessy beamed with delight as she read the list. 'Gaven is going to be pleased when he sees this. He'll probably have the demos videoed so the clips can be put up on the castle's website. It could bring in extra interest to your businesses.'

This encouraged the ladies to show each other the clips they had up on their websites demonstrating their crafting techniques and discussing the things they made.

'Customers are always interested in seeing how I knit,' said Bee. 'I try to put up clips showing my techniques and my latest yarn.'

'I do the same with my embroidery,' Amy agreed.

'My latest quilting clips showing my new quilts being held up in the sunlight by the loch have been popular with my customers,' Aileen added.

Knightly peered at the clips they were showing on their phones. 'These are excellent. Even I've got a notion now to knit, quilt and sew.'

The ladies smiled, and Amy teased him. 'We'll maybe make a crafter of you yet.'

'You'll certainly make me a customer,' he said. 'I'll be buying knitwear for the winter, a gorgeous quilt, various items I didn't know I needed but want now. Including the textile art painting that reminds me of the castle's forest. I was walking through part of the estate today and those colours and texture remind me of it.'

'My textile painting is based on that,' Robin told him.

'There you go then,' he said in a confirming tone. He looked at one of Amy's framed embroideries in a hoop. The design had brightly coloured flowers with bees and butterflies embroidered on the white cotton fabric. 'And I wouldn't have considered having embroidery on my wall, but this is beautiful. I want this too. Oh, and, is that quilt in shades of blue still available?' he said to Aileen.

'Sorry, it's been sold,' said Aileen. 'But I'd be happy to make one for you.'

'Yes, please do that. I've been needing to add bits and pieces to my house in Edinburgh, but I've been so busy with my theatre work.' He smiled at Sylvia. 'And I've a notion to buy a needle felted robin. I love robins. I can picture him perched in my dressing room at the theatre of my next show, like a little lucky mascot, reminding me of the great time I had here with all of you.'

'Take him.' Sylvia handed the robin to Knightly.

'No, no, no, I'll buy the robin,' Knightly insisted.

Sylvia shook her head. 'I made him for fun. I didn't intend selling him.'

Knightly held the robin up and smiled. 'What a cheeky expression he's got with that wee beak. Thank you so much, Sylvia. He'll be treasured.'

The conversation swung back round to the videos, with several of the ladies saying that they thought their presentations sounded unsure.

'I wish I sounded more confident,' said Aileen. 'I was a bit nervous talking about my quilts when a video was made recently by the side of the loch. You can't see Fyn, but he was holding up my quilts while his brother, Gare, was filming me. Etta and Bee were there too.'

Bee showed him clips that were taken that day, including one where she was spinning yarn inside her cottage.

He looked at the clips that Etta had showing her knitwear.

Amy spoke up. 'I'd like to sound more confident when I'm explaining my embroidery work.'

Knightly sat the robin down and took a deep breath. 'It's all in the breathing. I really don't think any of you need to improve your verbal presentations. But if you want to up your game, just breathe deeper while keeping your posture more upright.' He demonstrated what he meant.

Eager for any advice from the actor, whose voice was rich and smooth, the ladies tried to follow his tips.

Knightly stood up. 'Can I have a volunteer? Ah, yes, Amy, thank you. Could you stand up?'

Amy laughed, not having volunteered at all, but willing to go along with the fun.

He began to show them tips to help with their presentations. 'I'm not an expert in making videos like you have, but there are ways to breathe to improve your stage presentation that may be of help to you.'

Etta nodded. 'Yes, we're interested.'

The eager faces listened and joined in while Knightly demonstrated. 'Breathe in deeply.'

Amy went along with his instruction.

'Keep your shoulders relaxed, your expression pleasant, eyes engaged with your audience.'

Amy felt herself tense up.

'Give your shoulders a little shake, ease off that tension, and start again,' he said calmly.

The others were having a go while they were seated.

'Your first few words should sound light, to engage interest,' he said. 'Then alter the inflection as you speak, to vary the tone and keep your audience's attention, and then finish on a light note with a smile.'

Knightly continued to instruct them, and soon the ladies were nodding, hearing themselves sound more relaxed and confident.

'It just takes practise,' Knightly added.

'I find my introductions sound less confident,' said Amy. 'Then when I start talking about my embroidery, I sound more assured.'

'That's why it's handy to start on a light note.' Knightly gestured outwards, as if acting on stage. 'Engage your audience. Speak clearly and with interest in your tone.'

Knightly was concluding his demonstration when Gaven and Walter peered in the function room. From reception, they'd heard the theatrical voice resonating out from the room and wondered what was going on. Knightly wasn't causing any disruption to the guests. They were just curious to see what the ladies and the actor were up to.

Unseen, Gaven and Walter overheard the actor announcing to the ladies...

'I've always loved knitting, quilting and sewing, and designing my own embroidery patterns.' Knightly smiled and sounded like he meant every word, showing them how to improve their presentations.

Walter whispered to Gaven. 'A multi–talented lad.'

'Our guests are just full of surprises,' Gavin said in a hushed tone.

Nodding to each other, they then slipped back through to reception to attend to the guests and organise dinner for the ladies, and Knightly.

CHAPTER FOUR

Neil took advantage of Penny being away at the castle, and tested out the strands of twinkle lights in the garden. He got himself in a fankle with the twisted wires, but after managing to unravel the tangle, he hung them around the edges of the garden fence.

Switching them on and stepping back, he viewed the setting. Another few strands of lights were needed. He'd stocked up on enough to light up the village, so he dug out the extra strands and added them, like starlight sprinkled through the rose bushes and other flowers.

Neil nodded firmly. That's the fairytale effect he was looking for. Perfect. So perfect he was reluctant to undo all his work. He pondered whether to leave them there, unlit, until the engagement evening. It wasn't that long to keep them hidden in the flowers and foliage, and with them being clear bulbs and wires, Penny probably wouldn't even notice them.

He stood there wondering if this was feasible, and decided it was. He could discourage Penny from going into the back garden for a few days. It would be another important task tick boxed. Twinkle lights, diamond engagement ring, cake.

All he needed now was deciding what to cook for their engagement night dinner. He was a fine cook and Penny enjoyed the dinners he made. His savoury pie with puff pastry and roast potatoes seemed like a winner.

Plans made, he turned the lights off before anyone saw them. The back of the cottage was quite private, with only the rolling hillside beyond his garden.

No one saw Neil's light display, so his secret was safe.

Heading inside, he decided to work on Robin's ring, just in case Oliver needed it at short notice. In his experience, sometimes this happened. The best laid plans and all that... Besides, he'd done the hard work on the ring. The diamond was a scintillating success. The setting was almost finished. Now all he had to do was size it to fit Robin's finger and smooth off the edges to his usual perfect standard.

Sitting at his workbench, he sized, smoothed and finished the ring under the overhead spotlights. There was always a cosiness to nights like this, working quietly away.

When he'd first moved to the cottage, after taking a creative break at the castle, he knew he'd done the right thing leaving the city.

He'd been happy for a while, on his own, enjoying the tranquillity of his cottage, and the friendliness of the local community.

But then Penny, his new nearby neighbour, walked past his front garden one bright spring morning when he was cooking pancakes. He'd invited her in to join him, while telling her she could pick any flowers she wanted from his garden. She'd been looking at the colour of the flowers, the pansies and crocus, and counting the petals, planning the embroidery designs she used for her creative sewing and mending.

They'd had pancakes for breakfast in his kitchen, chatting easily as if they fitted right away in each other's company. They were still chatting, never stuck for conversation when they were together. The goldsmith and the sewing and mending expert. So different, and yet likeminded souls.

Now, here he was, planning to ask Penny to be his wife.

He glanced out the large window at the view of his lovely back garden and the starry night sky above the hillside beyond. He'd considered creating overarching lights across the garden, but nothing could beat nature's night skies sprinkled with thousands of stars.

There was a feeling in the air, he was sure of it. Maybe all the stars for Penny and him were finally aligning.

'Neil and I are in no hurry to take our romance to the next level,' Penny said to Robin. They were sitting in the castle's function room having tea and discussing their plans for autumn and Christmas.

'It's the same with Oliver and me,' Robin confided. 'We're both sooo busy, especially now that Oliver has his new book deal. Or should I say, three–book deal.'

'Neil hasn't even hinted about us settling down together,' said Penny.

'Neither has Oliver.'

'I'm thinking we'll discuss it in the spring. I met Neil in the spring, and my memory of that first day when he cooked me pancakes is etched in my mind forever.'

'Spring is a lovely time to...you know...get engaged.' Robin kept her voice down.

'It is. All those spring flowers.' Penny pictured it clearly. 'The colours of the autumn are gorgeous too.'

'Maybe Oliver and I will take things further next autumn,' said Robin.

Penny nodded.

Robin kept her voice to a confiding whisper. 'I'm wondering if Fyn will pop the question to Aileen soon. Apparently, they've fancied each other for a while, but only just started dating when Fyn felt confident that Aileen liked him.'

'They're a nice couple, well–suited I think.' Penny glanced over at Sylvia. 'Etta says things are really hotting up with Sylvia and Laurie.'

'Oh, yes. My money is on Sylvia and Laurie announcing their engagement next,' said Robin.

Careful not to be overheard by Aileen or Sylvia, they changed the subject to a safer topic.

'I hear you're going away soon to do one of your knitwear modelling magazine shoots,' Penny said to Robin.

'I am, not long after the fair. I'll only be away for a few days, but the planning takes in most of the week leading up to it and then settling back in and catching up with my textile art when I get back. Oliver says he'll keep an eye on my cottage until I get back,' said Robin.

'I've a short trip to Edinburgh after the fair to meet clients interested in my sewing and mending designs on vintage clothing. Then Neil's away on a separate weekend on his goldwork business to Edinburgh,'

Penny added. 'But absence makes the heart grow fonder, so they say.'

'It does. I'll miss Oliver when I'm away to Edinburgh after the fair.' Robin sighed. 'And I've been so busy lately creating textile art pieces to display at the fair.'

'Maybe we'll all find time to relax at Christmas,' Penny joked.

Robin scoffed. 'Hardly, according to Etta and the others, the year just gets busier in the winter months. We have the winter fair to plan next.'

Penny nodded. 'That's right. And the Christmas ball at the castle.'

'Spring and autumn next year are looking like the only times we'll have to relax,' said Robin.

'That's for sure,' Etta agreed, overhearing them. 'Though there's rarely a time here when there's not something exciting happening.'

Jessy showed the ladies the overall layout for the stalls in the main marquee. 'Etta and Aileen will have the same stall positions they had last year, as will others. But new local attendees, like Penny, Robin, Sylvia and Bee have stalls in excellent positions. And I've done the same for Elspeth, Kity and Amy.'

Amy was pleased to see that her stall was in a handy spot near the other ladies.

It was obvious that Jessy had been fair to everyone.

'I've tried to separate similar stalls so there's no sense of competing against each other. If anyone wants to change where I've put them, speak up, and I'll do my utmost to relocate you.'

The ladies studied the plan and everyone was happy with Jessy's suggestions.

Jessy smiled. 'Great, so do you have any questions about setting up your stalls? Walter and I will be there along with other staff to help you with anything you need.'

Oliver sat on the comfy, floral chintz couch in his living room trying to concentrate on sketching a bumblebee.

He lived comfortably above the art shop and often worked in the evenings upstairs, creating the artwork for the little characters in his picture books. Bees, butterflies, dragonflies, wasps, ladybirds and other cute creatures featured in the stories.

But he'd wound himself up, thinking about the engagement ring, and the proposal.

He put his sketch pad and pencil aside and gazed out the front window that had a view of the main street and the starry night sky.

The engagement ring was a sparkling success. He was sure of that. What a beautiful ring. But what if Robin didn't say yes? What if she wanted to wait until later in the year, or even next year, or never?

He got up and tried to shake the doubts away. He felt sure that Penny would accept Neil's proposal. They looked like such a happy and well–matched couple.

Unable to untwist the knot that was forming in his core, he flicked the main lights off in the living room, leaving only a solitary lamp illuminating the watercolours hanging on the walls. No decor issues for the man who could paint up whatever he needed to create scenery in his cosy flat.

Sometimes he'd hang a new painting up, having put photos of it for sale on his website. It helped give him ideas for other paintings, but often it was difficult to part with ones that had become favourites.

One large floral watercolour he'd kept because Robin loved it too. She'd admired it the night he'd invited her upstairs for a cup of tea. She liked the colours of the roses, jasmine, freesia, cornflowers and gerbera daisies in the painting.

He'd made them tea and hot buttered toast, and told her about the artwork for his picture books. They'd sat together on the couch talking about his books and her textile art. And fell asleep somewhere in the chatter, not waking up until the morning. They laughed about it now, but he remembered them scrabbling around and running downstairs when they realised they'd slept in and he needed to open his shop.

So much had happened since then, and now...the ring was in the making and...he needed to calm down.

His boots thundered down the wooden stairs, into the art shop where the display lights lit up the paintings in the front window.

Unlocking the door, he headed out, taking the route up to the loch.

A golden hour sky reflected over the loch as the last of the gloaming shimmered above the distant hills. Far beyond the forest at the end of the loch, where the road wound its way up to the castle, he could see the turrets peering over the trees.

He hoped Robin was enjoying her evening at the castle. The thought of her melted his heart every time. Even after these wonderful romantic months they'd had together, unlike the golden glow over the loch, his feelings for her refused to fade in the slightest.

If anything, he loved Robin more as time went on.

Oliver ran his hands through his hair, pushing it back from his troubled brow. No one was around to see him, and if they did, watching him from a window of a cottage, they'd assume he was out looking at the scenery for his artwork. His profession covered a multitude.

In the past, he'd often hid behind his art, but there was no hiding now, not when Neil was probably adding the finishing touches to the diamond ring for Robin. If only she knew...

Breathing in the calm evening air, fragrant with the scent of the greenery around the loch, he told himself that he just had a touch of the collywobbles and that Robin would accept his proposal.

Feeling better, he walked a full lap of the loch, seeing lights on in a few of the cottage windows. Less than usual, due to Robin, Penny, Etta and others being away at the castle. Robin had turned the outside lantern on to give a glow to the front door of her cottage.

It was a lovely mild night, and the fresh air certainly soothed his ragged senses as he walked along the edge of the loch.

For a moment, he thought he saw a twinkling glow from around Neil's cottage. He blinked, and it had gone. A trick of the light and his over active imagination, he thought.

Time to head back, make himself a mug of hot chocolate, and finish sketching that bumble.

Neil told himself he was a fusspot. Taking the scolding he gave himself, he stopped fiddling with the twinkle lights in the garden.

Don't turn them on again, he urged himself. Someone will see the glow. The lights are fine. The garden will look like a magical wonderland for his special night with Penny.

Heading back into his cottage, Neil put the kettle on for a cup of tea, and opened a fancy tin of shortbread.

Munching on a piece of Bradoch's special butter shortbread, he wondered if he should make Penny a bracelet or necklace to go with her ring.

He shook the thought away. The ring should be the highlight. The most beautiful diamond floral cluster set in yellow gold he'd ever made. There was only one person he'd made it for. The love of his life, Penny.

Lights glowed from Bradoch's bakery, shining out on to the main street.

The heart–shaped sponge cake and the round, traditional sponge were cooling on racks in the kitchen.

Bradoch didn't have any special cakes on order. He'd made the birthday and anniversary cakes, and they were due to be picked up soon. And he wanted to make sure the two engagement cakes would be ready sooner rather than later in case the proposal plans changed.

He loved baking cakes, and he particularly enjoyed icing them, decorating them with royal icing, utilising his years of skill in sugar craft.

While the sponges cooled, Bradoch prepared the fondant to create the flowers — and the engagement ring. He'd made an engagement ring and wedding ring before, though not for a long time, so he was prepared to have a few attempts to get it just right.

Surprising himself, he got the shape of the diamond ring spot on first time. A happy fluke he told himself, rather than take praise that he really was a skilled baker.

Dinner was being served to the ladies and Knightly in the function room. Catering staff deftly set the tables with napkins and cutlery.

Walter was there to give the ladies and their guest a message. 'Chef hopes you enjoy his new recipe lentil and vegetable soup, with a mix of his special spices for the autumn menu.'

'It smells delicious,' said Knightly.

'I can thoroughly recommend it,' Walter said with a grin, patting his firm stomach.

Baskets of thick–cut slices of farmhouse bread were placed on the tables, along with butter, salt and pepper.

'Chef thought you'd like a wee dish of tatties as a tasty extra,' Walter added.

Staff served up individual bowls of piping hot mashed potatoes sprinkled with greentails and a sprig of parsley to accompany their soup and bread.

'Tuck in,' Walter told them.

'Thank chef from all of us, Walter,' said Jessy.

Walter smiled. 'And there's a slice of apple pie and hot custard for afters.'

The ladies' faces lit up.

'What a treat,' said Knightly. 'I love mashed potatoes.'

'I'll be sure to put a bag of our local tatties, fresh from the farm, in your grocery delivery,' Walter assured him.

Having scooped up a mouthful of mash, Knightly gave Walter the thumbs up.

Tucking in, helping themselves to the tatties and bread, the happy gathering continued to chat about the fair and their various crafts.

Knightly enjoyed joining in, without having to discuss the drama in his life, and not all of it was on stage. Romance was a distant hope that kept getting dashed amid his busy theatrical work schedule. His life, he concluded, tended to be one big carousel of drama. Somewhere on the circuit of broken romantic dreams, he felt the urge to jump off and live a life less complicated.

Looking around at the cheery faces, at home with his newfound friends, feeling welcome for himself rather than as the successful actor, maybe it was coming up time to make the leap off the merry–go–round.

Etta scolded Knightly with a smile. 'You've got a faraway look in your eyes. Relax and enjoy your dinner. And grab another slice of that bread while it's still there.'

Knightly's smile lit up his own heart, as well as Etta's. He lifted another thick slice to eat with his soup and tatties. 'Cheers, Etta.'

She smiled back at him, and then the chatter continued with Knightly joining in.

For all the lavish dinners he'd had in the past months, this was the tastiest and most wholesome he'd had in a long time. He was beginning to see the reasons for the playful warnings he'd received, that he'd need to be careful not to fall in love with the village, or he'd never want to go home to the city.

Knightly glanced over at Amy.

Sensing him looking at her, she glanced back at him and smiled while eating her dinner.

His heart jolted again, like the first time he'd seen her. It had been a long time since a woman had caused such a potent reaction in him. Was the attraction mutual? He wasn't sure. Amy didn't treat him as if he was a celebrity, or was impressed by his personal wealth.

He continued to eat his dinner.

'Sorry to interrupt,' Gaven said hurriedly, approaching Knightly. 'Just a quick question.'

Knightly looked up and nodded, still munching on a chunk of bread and butter.

'Could you be persuaded to give a special display of your crafting prowess if Walter built a small stage for you in the main marquee?' Gaven looked hopeful.

Knightly seemed the amenable sort. And the ladies had obviously taken him under their wings.

Knightly took a swig of his tea to wash down the combination of guffaw and being gobsmacked.

'Knitting, quilting, showing how you design your embroidery patterns,' Gaven prompted him. 'I was talking to Struan from the Christmas Cake Chateau, and telling him about your hidden talents. He suggested highlighting you on our website. The film actors visiting his hotel stirred up a lot of interest in his chateau. With your theatrical experience it could create quite a sensation. We even have a contact on one of the popular radio shows. Mullcairn himself. What do you say?'

Knightly gulped down another mouthful of tea and then replied, trying to sound tactful. 'Under other circumstances, I'd love to. It's a great idea. There's only one little problem...'

CHAPTER FIVE

'Could you even stuff a felted robin?' Gaven said to Knightly.

'Oh that I could.' Knightly meant every word.

Gaven glanced at the ladies. 'Could Knightly be taught to craft something, anything, knit a pair of socks?'

'Difficulty level eleven,' said Etta.

'Right.' Gaven reconsidered. 'Stitch a tea cosy?'

'Better, but still a nine,' Jessy estimated.

'Okay,' said Gaven. 'We're going in the right direction.'

'Will I tell chef that the ladies and Knightly are ready for their puddings?' Walter said to Gaven.

'Yes, and lavish on the custard and cream. I think we're going to need it.' Never one to be easily thwarted by dire circumstances, Gaven was in full *we can find something Knightly can make* mode.

He had a room full of expert crafters and an actor willing to give it a go. There had to be a creative compromise in there somewhere. Digging deep, Gaven came up with an almost feasible solution. 'Can Knightly be taught something basic, on a scale of an impressive one or one and a half?'

Amy spoke up. 'I could teach him to embroider autumn acorns, using satin stitch and whipped back stitch.'

For a second, Knightly winced, thinking whipping and his back was involved, then realising it was the names of embroidery stitches, he relaxed.

Gaven looked hopeful. 'What do you say, Knightly? Are you up for demonstrating how you embroider your acorns?'

Learning how to embroider acorns from Amy didn't sound too bad, Knightly thought, brightening up. 'Okay, I'm game.'

'Good man,' Gaven said, delighted. 'We won't pull the wool over anyone. We'll be upfront and say that you're learning to craft. Right, I'll leave you in the capable hands of the ladies, and tell Walter to build a little stage.' And off he went.

'Did I just agree to make a complete fool of myself, in public, at the craft fair?' Knightly said to the ladies.

No one wanted to confirm this.

Etta had a suggestion. 'What if you thought about this from a whole different angle?'

'I'm listening,' said Knightly.

'Think of this as a role you've been given for a theatre play,' Etta told him. 'And now you have to prepare to get into character. Don't you ever have to learn new skills to play specific parts on stage?'

Knightly's world clicked into focus. 'I do. I had to learn how to juggle for dramatic effect once. And do an authentic–looking Highland Fling. I gave it such gusto, wardrobe had to add weights to my sporran to keep it hanging properly.'

'Well then,' said Etta. 'A wee bit of embroidery will be a skoosh in comparison.'

Knightly was inclined to agree. He glanced at Amy for her reaction.

Amy nodded encouragingly. 'Etta's right. I could give you the first lesson tomorrow, if you're not busy.'

'It's a date. A lesson date,' he corrected himself.

They exchanged phone numbers.

'Call me if you chicken out,' said Amy.

'No, I've plucked up the courage to give it a go,' he said.

Amy smiled. 'I'll come round to your cabin after breakfast.'

Knightly nodded firmly. Then he reconsidered. 'Have breakfast with me at the castle.'

They agreed to meet at nine for breakfast.

A trolley rattled as the puddings were wheeled through. Walter accompanied the catering staff as the generous dishes were served up.

Knightly looked at his slice of apple pie, custard and cream. 'Chef has been lavish with the whipped cream. Not that I'm complaining.' He playfully dug his spoon into the cream. 'I'm sure there's pie underneath here somewhere. Ah, yes, here it is.' He ate a mouthful, trying not to laugh.

The ladies' portions were equally generous, with spirals of whipped cream topping.

Amid the laughter and spluttering, they all enjoyed their puddings and each other's company.

Aileen was giggling and joking with Knightly as he balanced a huge piece of pie and cream on his spoon, when Fyn walked in.

The tall, fit, blond–haired figure, clad in snug–fitting denims, and carrying a single, long stem red rose, stood there assessing the situation. His light blue eyes looked right through Knightly, unable to hide the pang of uneasiness he felt seeing Aileen all but flirting with the handsome stranger.

'This is Knightly, a new guest at the castle. A stage actor from Edinburgh on a break in one of the cabins,' said Jessy, sensing the friction in the air. 'And this is Fyn. He owns the flower shop in the main street.'

Fyn wasn't usually the jealous type, and he didn't even consider this when it came to Aileen. She wasn't the type to play with his emotions or those of others. But still...he couldn't help feeling protective of his relationship with Aileen. Things were finally going well between them. The last thing he needed was a handsome actor on the scene.

Fyn nodded acknowledgement to the actor.

Knightly returned the nod in kind.

Feathers were clearly ruffled.

Fyn looked at Aileen. 'I was dropping off flowers for Gaven. I wondered if you'd like a lift home when you've finished your evening here.'

Fyn had dropped Aileen off at the castle before driving to the family farm to talk to his brother, Gare.

The ladies often gave each other a lift to and from the bee nights at the castle.

'Yes, but we're still having our dinner,' said Aileen.

'There's no rush. None at all. I've things to talk to Gaven about for the flowers for the fair. I just wanted to let you know I'm here.' He twirled the rose between his fingers, unsure whether to give it to her now or wait until later. Under the circumstances, he decided to wait.

'Knightly is going to be demonstrating his embroidery skills at the fair,' said Jessy. 'Amy, my niece, is planning to teach him.'

'Nice to meet you, Amy,' said Fyn. Then he got ready to walk away. 'I'll be through chatting to Gaven and Walter at reception, Aileen. And if any of you ladies want a lift too, I'd be happy to take you with us.'

'I'll take you up on that offer,' said Etta.

Another member accepted as well.

Smiling, Fyn left them to continue their evening.

Aileen finished her pudding and then said lightly, 'I'll be back in a wee minute.' She headed through to reception to talk to Fyn.

Another round of tea was served up to the ladies and Knightly as their plates were cleared away.

Amy explained to Knightly what she'd teach him so he wouldn't lose any sleep over the thought of his first lesson.

They'd just finished talking about this, when Aileen came back into the function room, all smiles and carrying the rose. She made no comment, and no one pried, but whatever tension there had been was now gone.

The embroidery chat picked up again.

'Satin stitch sounds nice and smooth,' said Knightly.

'It is,' Amy told him. 'It's a beautiful stitch to learn. You'll begin by learning how to satin stitch part of an acorn. I think you'll pick it up in no time.'

Knightly frowned. 'What about the whipped back stitch?'

Amy had brought her craft bag with her. She took out a six inch embroidery hoop and a piece of white cotton that was larger than the hoop. Putting the fabric tightly into the hoop, she handed it to Knightly along with a fine–tip pencil.

'Sign your name on the fabric,' Amy said to Knightly. 'Write light, easy and clear.'

'I've never written on fabric before,' he said, doing his best to make it neat. He then handed the hoop back to Amy.

'Ideal,' she said, cutting a length of six–stranded embroidery thread. She threaded a needle with two strands of thread. 'We'll work with two strands to give substance to the stitches. Watch how I bring the needle up through the back of the fabric in the hoop, and then back down, making a small stitch on the start of your name on the pencil line.'

Knightly sat beside her, keen to learn.

'Now I bring the needle and thread back up here to create the back stitch. Basically, the stitches double back on each other. This creates a single line of small stitches with no gaps in between. Want to try?'

Knightly let Amy guide his hands, feeling the gentle touch of her fingers on his. He concentrated on learning, getting the technique right. It made sense. Stitching along the signature. Her stitches were neat. His were messy, a bit wobbly, but he understood the theory. He just needed to practise. And he was prepared to do that.

'You pick things up quickly,' Amy said to him.

Knightly shrugged. He did. He'd always been sharp and keen to give things a go.

The ladies watched Knightly work one stitch at a time.

'You could demonstrate how to embroider your signature at the fair,' Jessy suggested.

'I like that idea,' Knightly said, continuing to work his way along the pencil mark. 'The thread covers the pencil line.'

'That's right,' said Amy. 'And you could leave it like that, as a back stitch embroidered name. But once you've finished that, and it'll take you a wee while, then I'll show you how to add the whipped stitch to it.'

Knightly wondered if this was the difficult part.

'That's the easy part because the whipped stitches are slipped under the back stitches. Not through the fabric.' Amy showed him pictures on her phone of the whipped back stitch.

'Oh, I get it,' Knightly said, sussing out what he was supposed to be doing. 'It's like entwining the back stitches with thread.'

'Yes, it creates a lovely effect for stems, leaf designs, all sorts of outlines, like your name here. You can use the same colour or two different colours.'

'Can I take this embroidery with me to practise and try to finish the back stitches?' said Knightly.

Amy nodded. 'I'll give you the skein of embroidery thread. And another colour.' She showed him how to cut a length of the embroidery thread and separate the strands. 'Use two strands, and don't have your thread too long or it will knot and fankle.'

'I'll use the strands you've cut. I can thread a needle and stitch a button on my shirt, but that's the extent of my sewing skills,' Knightly admitted.

'That's all you need. Phone if you get stuck. We'll continue the lesson in the morning. Take this with you too. It's a needle book. Tuck your needle inside it to keep it safe.'

Knightly opened the little handmade book. It was made of cotton fabric and pieces of felt. The cotton book cover was quilted, padded with wadding, and embroidered. Inside it had a couple of felt pages where several needles were stored. 'Keep your needle in your book when you're not using it.'

'Did you make this?' Knightly liked it.

'I did.'

'I'll keep it safe,' he promised.

Amy gave him a paper bag to put it in along with his thread and embroidery hoop.

Knightly put his needle in the book, closed it and tucked everything in the bag. 'Kitted out and set to go.'

The ladies got ready to leave having made great headway with their plans for the fair.

Knightly walked beside Amy as they all headed through to reception where Gaven and Walter were behind the desk.

Sean, one of the local beemasters, a fine–looking man in his fifties with light brown hair, was waiting to give Muira a lift home to her cottage near the loch. They'd recently started dating. Muira had arrived in Sylvia's car, but her niece intended going to see Laurie, her boyfriend.

Laurie was still staying in his luxury cabin in the castle's estate while a local house he'd recently purchased was being refurbished to include a home recording studio for his music.

Sean was so much taller than Muira that she had to stand on her tiptoes to return the welcoming kiss he gave her. Wrapping his arm around her shoulders, Sean swept Muira away.

As everyone got into the cars, sharing lifts home, Amy set off down the flower–bordered path to walk to Jessy's cottage. Her aunt was continuing to work at the castle, and wouldn't be finished until later.

Knightly hurried to catch up with Amy. 'Can I walk you home?'

'I'm fine. I know my way. The path leads through the trees right to Jessy's cottage and everything's lit with solar lights, so I won't get lost in the forest or anything like that. No trail of breadcrumbs required.'

'I insist,' said Knightly. 'My cabin is nearby anyway.' He walked beside her, that towering figure becoming more familiar to her each time they strolled along together.

He breathed deeply. 'The air is so clear here.'

Amy tilted her head to look up at the stars. 'The skies are clear too. My town is like this, but I love the feeling of walking through a fairytale forest estate with a castle in the heart of it.' She glanced back at the castle, the windows aglow with lights.

'It's perfect,' he said.

'Sylvia says her boyfriend, Laurie, the singer and musician, is living in one of the cabins until a property he's purchased in the village is refurbished and ready.'

'I know Laurie,' Knightly revealed. 'I've met him a few times at parties in Edinburgh.'

'The celebrity party circuit must be fun, though I'm more of a homebody.'

'Surely you like to party sometimes.'

'I do,' she admitted. 'But most of my friends in the town are dating, engaged or married nowadays, and it's not in my nature to go out to parties on my own or as a third wheel.'

'Come to parties with me in Edinburgh. I'll show you a wild time.'

'I just bet you would,' Amy scoffed at him. 'You're trouble.' And temptation, though she kept the latter label to herself.

He grinned, causing her heart to flutter. 'The okay type of trouble.'

'Is there such a thing?'

'In my world there is.'

'I'm the sensible sort and not inclined to invite trouble into mine.'

He brushed a low–hanging branch out of her way as they continued along.

'Leading us back to what you told me before. You've always dated the wrong men, even when they seemed not the troublemaker type.'

He had her pinned on that one. 'I'm happy with the way things are in my world.' Her amethyst eyes sparkled in the nightglow.

Knightly didn't believe her. Deep down, he knew she didn't believe this either. He let this part of their conversation filter out into the calm night.

Jessy's pretty cottage came into view. 'This is my aunt's cottage.'

Two lanterns lit the front door, and it was hard to tell where her garden ended and the greenery of the estate began. Merging into one verdant niche, the cottage had a homely quality, and Amy was enjoying living there even if it was only for a little while.

'I'll wait until you're safely in,' he insisted.

Amy walked up the garden path, unlocked the door and then called to him. 'Don't get lost in the forest on your way back.'

Knightly smiled and waved. 'I won't, but I'll phone you if I need rescued.' And off he went.

Amy stood at the doorway, lit by the glow of the lamps, watching the tall troublemaker, with his bag of embroidery, walk away into the trees and disappear.

Something in her heart ached, just for a second, taking her aback.

Shaking off the sense of longing, she went inside the cottage and closed the door on a day and night she'd always remember. When she'd met Knightly, the actor, the man inviting her to go wild with him in Edinburgh.

Jessy's cottage was beautifully traditional, and over the years she'd styled it in so many different ways that it was now an eclectic mix of home comfort and a crafter's dream home.

The living room extended into the garden, and the garden itself extended into the forest, so Jessy's decor had lots of floral prints on the cushions, couch covers and comfy chairs. A sewing machine was set on a table beside a dresser with shelves containing Jessy's fabric stash and knitting.

Quilts were folded tidily on chairs and the couch, and the large kitchen had a mix of modern appliances and vintage styling. Amy enjoyed cooking, and that thought of giving Knightly a homemade dinner crossed her mind again as she made herself a cup of tea to settle whatever the adventurous actor had stirred in her.

Lamps created a warm glow to the living room, and a log fire was set ready for whenever the weather decided to be cold enough to merit it. So far, the autumn evenings were mild, and Amy padded around in her socks

Getting ready for bed, she couldn't shake off how much his offer appealed to her, and scolded herself. Look at the heartache she'd endured avoiding dating troublemakers. Imagine the double heart break if she took a man like Knightly up on his offer.

Penny and Robin had stayed back to have a proper look through the photo album. Over another cup of tea, they sat in the function room, just the two of them, studying the stalls from various years.

'Look at the lovely fabric draped over the back of this quilting stall a few years ago,' said Penny.

Robin peered at it. 'I like that idea. And see how it's tied with ribbons to hold the fabric in place. Such a nice touch.'

'The knitting stalls are so pretty with all their colourful yarn,' Penny remarked. 'Do you think you should emphasise that you're a knitwear model as well as a textile artist?'

'I'd never thought of this, but it could add an extra element of interest in my stall.'

'I'm hanging up a selection of garments that I've sewn and mended with crewel wool and embroidery thread.' She indicated one of the photos. 'See how that stall has rails of vintage clothes.'

'Are they taking part this year?' said Robin.

'No, that was several years ago. This album is a goldmine of information and ideas for our stalls.'

Drinking their tea, unaware of the time, they continued to be steeped in chatter looking through the photos.

Neil put Robin's ring in a velvet jewel box and tucked it in the safe. It was finished. He sent a message to Oliver, not expecting a reply this late at night:

Oliver, it's ready.

Neil didn't add any hint of what it was in case Robin saw the message by mistake.

Flicking the overhead lamps off in his workshop, Neil headed outside to his front garden to see if the main lights were on in Penny's cottage. As he peered along to where her cottage was situated, on the same side of the loch as him, it was in darkness. He assumed she was still at the castle, or on her way home.

Unsettled, he stood in the garden and gazed out across the loch. Not long now until it was the evening of his proposal. His heart thundered every time he thought about it. Not from trepidation or second thoughts. Not at all. He wished he could march across to her cottage that evening, when she arrived home, and propose that night.

He wouldn't though, but it was a wild thought. He'd never been wild in his entire life, he admitted to himself, unsure if this was of merit or a minus.

Before he could decide, he received a reply from Oliver:

Fast work, Neil. I'll pop round in the morning.

Then another message came through from Oliver:

Is Penny home yet from the castle?

No, I'm in the garden looking at her cottage. It's in darkness.

Can you see if the lights are on in Robin's cottage?

Neil checked. *Nope. I guess they're still having a nice time.*

Oliver phoned Neil. 'Robin messaged me earlier saying a well–known stage actor, Knightly, had joined the ladies for dinner at the castle. He's on one of the creative breaks like we had. I checked him out online.'

'What does he look like?'

'Film star material. Around the same age as us, just a lot more...theatrical.'

'A potential troublemaker?' Neil sounded wise but wary.

Oliver sent a link to Knightly's website.

Neil clicked on it and balked when he saw the actor's handsome face peering out. 'He's the man I saw outside Bradoch's bakery flirting with Penny and the ladies. Robin wasn't there though.' Neil studied the face. Oh, yes, that was the smile of a troublemaker if ever he'd seen one.

'Are you up for a stealth excursion to the castle?' said Oliver.

'Yes.'

'I'm on my way.' Oliver ended the call, grabbed his car keys, hurried out of the art shop and drove to Neil's cottage. It took all of three minutes max.

Neil was waiting at the garden gate and jumped into the car.

Oliver took off up the forest road.

'I trust Penny implicitly,' Neil insisted.

'I feel the same about Robin. But did you see that confident smile on Knightly's face?'

Neil felt an unfamiliar stab of jealousy through his heart. The thought that Penny could be taken in by this man's confidence burned like a hot knife.

'We're probably overreacting because we're wound up about the proposals.' Neil tried to sound calm.

'I think you're right,' Oliver agreed. 'I know fine that I'm in jackrabbit mode, but a peek at the situation seems sensible.'

Sensible and what they were doing didn't match. But tonight, Neil was okay with that. Maybe deep, deep inside, he could be a troublemaker too.

Oliver drove through the open gate entrance to the castle. 'I'll park under the trees so we're not on show.'

Getting out of the car, the two well–behaved, potential troublemakers, scurried in the pockets of shadows and light up to the front entrance to the castle and peered inside. They saw Gaven, Walter and Jessy at the reception desk.

'Jessy's there,' Neil said, his voice an urgent hiss. 'She organised the get together this evening. Why does she look like the evening's over? She seems to be checking the bookings with the laird.'

Oliver scanned the cars parked out front. 'Robin's car is parked over there.'

'So is Penny's car,' said Neil.

'And that one belongs to Sylvia,' Oliver added, knowing it well from seeing it parked across the street from him outside the sweet shop. 'But she spends a lot of time with Laurie at his cabin.'

'True.'

Penny and Robin finally headed out of the function room, chatting as they walked through reception. Walter had headed away, but Gaven and Jessy were still at the reception desk.

Oliver and Neil heard the familiar voices of Penny and Robin.

'Here they come now,' Oliver warned Neil.

'Should we run, hide or other?' Neil didn't know what option three entailed.

'What are you two scallywags up to sneaking about in the shadows?' Walter said taking them by surprise.

'Nothing,' Oliver lied.

Neil nodded.

Walter wasn't daft. 'You'd better not let your lassies see you skulking around, checking up on them. Come on, hurry up, before they see you.'

CHAPTER SIX

'I can see fine that the two of you are in cahoots,' Walter whispered as the three of them hid in the greenery outside the castle watching the front entrance.

Oliver glanced at Neil. Their faces were highlighted by the glow from the castle. They exchanged a knowing look. They could trust Walter.

Neil wasn't the type to get up to mischief. He'd never skulked about in the bushes. It didn't suit him.

Oliver couldn't say the same about himself. Not entirely. Collywobbles wasn't an excuse for a furtive excursion. He nodded to Neil.

'Only three of us know what we're planning,' Neil began.

Walter frowned. 'I don't know.'

'Bradoch knows our secrets.' Neil revealed the details of what they were planning.

'I sensed it was something to do with romance,' said Walter. 'I've seen lots of guests over the years, couples planning to get engaged, married, and the pair of you had that look about you.' He frowned again. 'But it sounds like you've got your rings and cakes sorted out, so what's got your feathers in a fluff?'

'The actor,' said Oliver. 'Knightly.'

'Aye, right, I get it now,' said Walter. 'He ruffled Fyn's feathers tonight. Fyn walked into the function room to talk to Aileen. He'd brought her a rose, and found her giggling as Knightly played around with the whipped cream on his custard and apple pie pudding.'

As they lingered in the lamplight, Walter told them the gist of what happened. 'Aileen smoothed his feathers and everything's hunky–dory now.'

'Is Knightly a troublemaker?' Neil said outright to Walter. 'He's barely here a day and he's caused commotion in the community.'

'No,' Walter said considering how to explain the trouble magnet in the newcomer. 'But he brings a sense of drama with him. The ladies like him. He's a cheery character. The only one that Jessy and I think he's romantically interested in is her niece, Amy.'

'I don't know Amy,' said Oliver.

Neither did Neil.

'Amy lives in a wee town nearby, but she's staying with Jessy while she takes part in the craft fair. She's an embroiderer,' said Walter.

'So, Knightly's just a jinx for drama,' Oliver suggested.

Walter nodded. 'Aye, he's an okay lad. Gaven's roped him in to give a demonstration of embroidery at the craft fair. Folk love a bit of celebrity. Knightly's now learning how to embroider acorns. He's here on holiday to relax and recharge his batteries, but now he's part of the fair's performance. I've to build a wee stage for him.'

'Knightly's part of the craft fair now?' Neil sounded surprised.

Walter nodded. 'Struan from the Christmas Cake Chateau further north suggested it to Gaven. They've been friends for years and help each other to promote their hotels and special events, especially for the autumn and Christmastime.'

Before Walter could continue, his phone rang. 'It's Sean, the beemaster,' he whispered to them. 'What's he wanting this time of night?'

'Walter,' Sean's strong, confident voice rang out clear from the phone. 'I know it's late, but I saw on the castle's website that you're on night duty at the castle.'

'I am, Sean. What's up? You sound perturbed,' said Walter.

'I need to get some sleep as I'm up early to tend to the beehives,' Sean began. 'But I can't settle. Do you know anything about an actor that's on holiday at the castle? Knightly.'

'I do.' Walter gave Sean the short course about Knightly. 'Why, what's wrong?'

'I came up to the castle tonight to give Muira a lift home,' Sean explained. 'All the way back, she spoke about Knightly this, Knightly that. I'm not jealous. I'm happy to romance Muira, and she didn't hint of anything like that. It's just...even when I dropped her off at her cottage and went in for a cup of tea, she spoke about Sylvia giving Knightly a felted robin. All the ladies seem to have gone starry–eyed for him.'

Oliver glanced worriedly at Neil as they could hear the conversation from Walter's phone outside in the quiet night.

'Knightly's certainly been a hit with the ladies,' Walter admitted.

'Muira says he had afternoon tea with them at Bradoch's bakery,' said Sean. 'Then he joined them for dinner at their crafting bee meeting tonight at the castle. What was he doing there? Apparently, he can't craft for toffee.'

'I'm not sticking up for Knightly,' Walter clarified. 'But the ladies invited Knightly to join them for soup and mashed tatties.'

'And pudding!' Sean added, sounding out of sorts.

'Calm yourself, Sean.'

'Aye, you're right. I've got a bee in my bonnet the night,' Sean admitted, lowering his tone from irate to mildly miffed.

'You're not the only man rankled because of Knightly,' Walter revealed.

Sean's calmness jumped up two scales to the wary zone. 'Other men in our village?'

Walter glanced at the furtive twosome. They gave him the nod. 'Oliver the artist, and Neil the goldsmith. And Fyn.'

'Deary me,' said Sean. Then he breathed deeply. 'I don't mean to sound obtuse, but that makes me feel better, that I'm not the only man worried we've got a cock of the walk in our community.'

'Don't be sorry, Sean,' Walter assured him. 'I've got your back. If Knightly oversteps, I'll sort him out. Now get some sleep. Besides, Knightly's got himself in a pickle having to learn embroidery. And there's a rumour that he's going to do a Highland Fling on stage at the fair. He's brought his kilt with him.'

Sean felt relieved. Muira didn't like blatant exhibitionists. 'Thanks again, Walter.' The call ended there on an easy note.

'Knightly's dancing at the fair!' Oliver sounded ratty. 'Burling around in his kilt. He'd better not be going commando.'

'No, certainly not,' Walter assured Oliver. 'And it's just a rumour. Probably crossed wires.'

Neil let rip with a snippy comment. 'What's Knightly going to do for an encore — sing or juggle?'

'I don't know if he can sing,' said Walter, sounding serious. 'But he said he learned to juggle for a theatre show he was in.'

Neil sighed heavily.

Before they could discuss the ructions caused by Knightly, they saw Penny and Robin coming out of the castle, chatting, and heading to their cars which were parked near each other.

A message popped up on Neil's phone from Penny:

I'm heading home. Had a great night at the castle. Lots of things planned for the fair. Penny. x.

Neil shared the message with Oliver and Walter.

Oliver checked to see if he had a message from Robin. Nothing. He looked downcast.

Walter nudged Oliver. 'Send a message to Robin.'

Oliver did:

Hope you had an enjoyable night. See you tomorrow. Love, Oliver. xx

Neil quickly typed a reply to Penny:

Come round for breakfast. I'll make pancakes. x, Neil.

A reply for Oliver popped up:

Love you too. Robin. x.

Oliver smiled as he read it, feeling all was right again with his world.

The final message showed up on Neil's phone:

Busy for breakfast and lunch. Pancakes for dinner? Penny. x.

Neil responded with a heavy heart:

It's a date. x, Neil.

From behind the three of them, a man's voice rang out. 'Can I help you find whatever you're looking for?' Knightly smiled helpfully at them. 'I brought a torch.' He turned it on. The beam lit them up like a beacon.

Neil shielded his eyes from the dazzling bright glare. 'Turn that off! You're lighting us up!'

Knightly, realising his helpful intentions had caused mischief, fiddled with the buttons on the torch. He'd seen them bumbling around in the bushes from the window of his cabin. Assuming they were looking for something in the dark, he'd rummaged around the kitchen cupboards and found a handy torch. Unfamiliar with the buttons, he pressed the wrong one again. The beam extended outwards, really illuminating them.

Penny shouted over to Robin as they were about to get into their cars to drive home.

'What's happening over there in the bushes?' Penny sounded concerned. 'Is that Walter? Does he need help?'

Pluckily running over to help Walter, Penny and Robin sprinted faster than the men anticipated.

Knightly struggled to find the right buttons. Why couldn't it just be an on and off switch. But no, it had more variety than some of the shows he'd been in. Another button he pressed changed the light to a flashing blue one. Handy for dancing in the dark, but hardly the effect he needed right now.'

With no time for any reasonable plan, Walter grabbed the torch, turned it off, and made the decision for them. 'Bluff and bluster, lads.'

Knightly responded instantly, as if receiving direction on stage. He plastered on a smile.

Walter tried to sound chirpy and carefree, a tricky combination considering the pickle they were in.

Oliver stared, blinking, still dazzled by the light.

Neil forced a grin that didn't match the situation.

Penny ran up to Neil. 'Is everything okay?' Clearly it wasn't.

'What are you all doing out here in the dark?' Robin said to Oliver.

Knightly replied first. 'I was helping Walter and his assistants. I pressed the wrong buttons on the torch. Fiddly fingers. My mistake, sorry for the razzle dazzle.'

Walter went for the full bluff and bluster response. 'The lads were helping me with the stage for the fair. The one Gaven wants me to build for Knightly. It's cumbersome to carry the pieces on my own, and so the lads were giving me a hand to lift the wood that's kept in the shed, to the store at the back of the castle near the rear entrance to the kitchen.'

Penny and Robin looked suitably confused, and yet, Walter always knew what was going on with the running of the castle's facilities.

'Why are you in the bushes, at the front of the castle?' said Robin.

'We dropped a piece,' Oliver muttered.

Neil nodded and pointed around him. 'A key piece.'

'We thought we'd located it when you arrived,' Knightly chipped–in.

Penny blinked. 'So where is it?'

Robin nodded, glancing around. There was nothing but greenery and a sense of mischief.

Walter brushed their concerns aside. 'I'll find it in the morning. It's just a wee widget.'

A message came through for Neil from Bradoch. At this time of night? He checked in case it was important:

I've made the fondant engagement ring for the cake. What do you think? Bradoch had taken a picture of it.

Neil sent a quick reply:

Perfect. Thanks, Bradoch.

Penny gave Neil a questioning look. 'Was that a photo someone sent you?'

'Yes, a picture of a ring,' said Neil. Not a lie, but wide of the truth.

Penny relaxed, assuming it was to do with his goldwork designs.

Walter rubbed his hands together. 'Right, it's getting a bit brisk. We should all call it a night. Away back to your cabin, Knightly.'

Knightly took the unsubtle hint. 'Goodnight.' He gave a pleasant wave and walked away.

'Thanks, for your assistance, lads,' Walter told Oliver and Neil.

'Happy to help,' said Oliver.

'Anytime,' Neil added.

Feeling there was a chance they'd bamboozled and blustered their way out of the sticky situation, Walter hurried back to the castle, while Neil walked Penny to her car.

Oliver accompanied Robin.

Penny looked around the car park. 'Where's your car?' she said to Neil.

'I gave him a lift,' Oliver chipped–in.

Penny nodded, piecing together the jigsaw that didn't quite seem to fit. But it had been a long day, a fun night, and it was late so... 'I'll give you a lift home,' she said to Neil.

Neil got in the passenger seat and Penny drove them away.

Robin and Oliver followed in their cars, down the forest road to the loch.

Penny had stopped being suspicious, but commented anyway. 'I thought staff at the castle would've helped Walter.'

'They'd gone home for the night.' Neil squirmed. He didn't like lying to her. 'Fyn was busy with Gaven, sorting the flower plans. Sean had left with Muira. So Walter phoned me and I phoned Oliver.'

'It was nice of the two of you to help Walter like that,' said Penny.

Neil smiled tightly and said nothing.

By now they'd reached the loch. Penny parked outside her cottage.

They got out of the car.

'See you tomorrow night,' said Neil, pulling her close for a goodnight kiss. 'Pancakes for dinner.'

'I'm sorry I'm busy during the day, but clients want samples of my mending designs, and I would've worked on them tonight. Instead I wanted to go to the castle.' She shrugged. 'A courier is collecting them late in the afternoon, if I finish them on time.'

'You will.' Neil kissed her, wishing he could tell her what he'd been up to. The plans for the engagement. One day he'd let her in on the secret.

Penny smiled, and headed into her cottage while Neil walked to his that was nearby.

Inside, he sighed with relief. Penny had no idea about the proposal. It had been a chaotic and crazy day, but he'd achieved what he'd planned to do — get Bradoch to make the cake, try out the twinkle lights, plan the proposal.

His feelings about Knightly being a menace had waned. The well–meaning fool had almost caused their plans to be ruined when he'd come to help them with that torch.

Now Walter knew his secret too, but considering what had happened at the castle, he was inclined to think the proposal plans were safe with him.

Weary from the rollercoaster of a day, Neil got ready for bed.

Robin parked outside her cottage, then ran over to Oliver's car as he waited to give her a goodnight kiss.

'Penny and I found lots of information and ideas in the castle's photo album of previous craft fairs,' Robin told him.

Oliver was happy to see the excitement in her, unaware of the chaos that had occurred. Feeling less anxious about the proposal, he drove off to his shop in the main street.

Robin waved, turned the outside lantern off, headed into her cottage, and went to bed.

Walter phoned Knightly. 'Thanks for going along with the chaos.'

'I'm used to being in the thick of it. Drama follows me around,' said Knightly. 'The two, well–heeled men, are they local residents?'

'Yes, Neil is a goldsmith. He's dating Penny. Oliver owns the art shop in the main street and he's dating Robin.'

'Ah, those are the men Amy mentioned to me earlier. Are you going to let me in on the skulduggery?'

'You don't want to know,' Walter told him.

Hearing Walter's tone, he decided he didn't. He'd created enough drama for one day. And managed to become a fledgling embroiderer in the process.

'I don't intentionally stir things up,' Knightly said defensively.

'Well, breakfast is served in the guests' dining room. Try to start the day without causing trouble for yourself or anyone else.'

'I haven't had a trouble–free day in a long while,' he joked.

'It's time you did then,' said Walter.

Fyn and Aileen lay on a quilt in the back garden of her shop, after he'd driven her home from the castle, and gazed up at the thousands of stars in the clear night sky.

Stargazing like this was something they'd discovered they loved to do, especially after a hectic day.

Aileen had turned the twinkle lights in her garden off, and they lay there pointing to their favourite stars and constellations.

Fyn clasped her hand and gave it a reassuring squeeze. 'I missed you today. I barely had a chance to talk to you.'

'We're both extra busy with the plans for the fair. Everyone in the village is. The lights were still on in Bradoch's bakery at this late hour. He's up at the crack of dawn. He must be snowed–under with special orders.'

'Most of the local businesses are. Gaven wants a lot of flowers for the marquees. I was discussing the designs. But they'll look lovely, and so will the stalls, especially one I know selling quilts.'

Aileen laughed. 'I did well with my stall at the fair last year. And there are some gorgeous new floral print fabrics I've used to make my quilts this time.'

'And I'll be there to give you a hand, if you need me.'

Aileen squeezed Fyn's hand. 'I certainly do.'

Lying there, they chatted about Aileen's quilts, Fyn's flowers, and everything in between, never short of conversation, only ever short of time. But they let the time drift that night, enjoying the late evening under the starry sky.

CHAPTER SEVEN

The early morning sunlight reflected off the window of the sweet shop. The jars of sweets, from barley sugar and lemon sherbets to brightly wrapped assorted toffees, glistened temptingly.

Sylvia and Muira were busy getting the shop ready for opening within the hour. They wore the pretty pink, sweetie print aprons that Aileen had made for them. Sylvia wore her blonde hair in a ponytail, and lately, Muira had added more style to her hair, pinning it up in a chignon with classy clasps rather than plain clips.

Since Muira had started dating Sean recently, Sylvia had noticed a bloom in her aunt's cheeks, and was happy for her and the beemaster.

The delicious scent of vanilla from the Scottish tablet filled the air. Sylvia made it with butter, sugar and condensed milk, and her new key ingredient — the beemasters' local honey. She'd cut the tablet in bite–size squares, that were like a creamy fudge. These would be wrapped ready for customers coming into the shop, and packaged for their online orders that were posted daily. Muira was an expert at wrapping the sweets, but she was currently busy refilling jars with traditional sweets and chocolates.

Muira had already wrapped the macaroon bars and chocolate truffles, while Sylvia was working in the kitchen. Sylvia lived in the cosy accommodation at the back of the shop that had a small garden with a shed. Living and working in a sweet shop was a dream come true for Sylvia. And now that she was dating Laurie, her life was starting to feel complete.

Their mornings were usually busy, but lately the castle's chef had ordered more sweets from the shop, particularly the Scottish tablet and honey nougat, another of Sylvia's new recipes.

Sylvia checked her recipe list. The treacle toffee was made and cooling in the kitchen, along with the chocolate robins. She cooked various confections throughout the day, and they sold a variety of sweets they bought wholesale. Her latest marzipan treats for the autumn had been popular, and she started to make the little marzipan rosy apples and pumpkins.

The previous evening at the castle had been fun. This would be her first craft fair, and she was going to share Muira's stall selling little needle felted robins, owls, foxes, fairies, toadstools and bumblebees. Knitted items, mainly made by Muira, such as cardigans and hat and scarf sets, would be on sale at their stall too.

Muira had attended the craft fair since it had started, and although the sweet shop was her main business, she loved taking part in the fair. It helped to promote the shop as well, and a selection of popular confections would be displayed along with the knitted items and needle felting.

One of Sylvia's felt robins was perched on a shelf in the shop, his eyes glaring as if guarding the premises from intruders with his cheeky attitude.

'Is Laurie coming to the fair?' Muira said to Sylvia as they worked in tandem.

Sylvia sighed. 'He's away that weekend singing and playing in Edinburgh. But he's hoping to drive back on the Sunday night in time for the craft fair dance at the castle.' She couldn't complain. They worked their schedules around each other's careers and there were times when they overlapped when Sylvia was involved in Laurie's music.

A trained classical pianist, she'd taken the village aback when they'd recently found out she had a secret talent, and had performed with Laurie at the opening of the castle's new piano bar, playing the beautiful baby grand piano Gaven had bought.

'I have the promotional banner for the stall wrapped up and stored in the garden shed,' Muira told Sylvia. 'I had it printed up a few years ago with the sweet shop's name and logo, and it's a pretty pink colour with splashes of sweeties.'

'It sounds eye–catching.' Sylvia wiped the marzipan from her fingers. 'I'm curious to see what it looks like. I'll be back in a wee minute.' And off she ran, out the kitchen door to the back garden and disappeared into the shed.

Rummaging around, she found it on one of the shelves above where Muira's pink bicycle was kept. Lately, Sylvia had been borrowing the pink bike to ride around the loch to unwind after a day's work at the sweet shop. The colder weather would soon curtail her exciting excursions that included cycling up the forest road to the castle's estate. Exploring the countryside, feeling the fresh air through her hair, had become one of her favourite joys, along with dating Laurie.

Unrolling part of the banner, Sylvia smiled seeing how pretty it looked, then stashed it away carefully again.

Heading back inside, she washed her hands before continuing making the marzipan sweets and chatting about the stall's presentation with Muira.

'The banner will look great across the stall,' Sylvia said as Muira came through for a refill of the nougat.

'Etta and Aileen have kept their banners and posters from past fairs. The stalls are always well set up for us in the marquees. We'll display our needle felted items on the main part of the stall, and hang up the cardigans and other knitwear. We're not like Etta and Aileen though. They've got lots of stock to sell. But it's fun to participate and I usually sell most of the things I make, and it promotes the sweet shop.'

'We'll need to think what we'll wear for the dance,' said Sylvia.

Muira nodded excitedly, and then took the nougat through to wrap it in the front shop, while Sylvia added tiny leaves to the marzipan apples and pumpkins.

Sunlight shone over Sean's large farmhouse style home in one of the fields where his son, Campbell, was tending to the beehives. Campbell, in his early thirties, was zipped up from head to toe in his white beekeeping suit, with a veil on his hood, and wearing white gauntlets.

In a corner of one of their fields was the old–fashioned cottage that Campbell was restoring so he could live in it. Having trained as a beemaster like his father, he'd recently come to stay with Sean to help with the honey–making.

Sean had poured his wealth into the farmhouse and surrounding fields, enjoying his life as a beemaster. He'd previously been a successful businessman and had made his money in finance in the city. But these past few years living in the village suited him.

Packing up his car with honey for the local deliveries, Sean waved to Campbell, smiling as a white gauntlet hand waved back, and then drove down to the main street. His first delivery was to Bradoch's bakery, and then to the sweet shop. He was looking forward to seeing Muira.

Bradoch worked on icing the engagement cakes in the bakery kitchen. He used a turntable to slowly spin the round sponge cake while he smoothed the icing on it. He loved tasks like this, and worked away, trying to get the first layer of icing finished before the shop got busy, as it always did when customers came in for their fresh morning rolls and bread.

The icing on the heart–shaped cake was finished to perfection. He'd outdone himself, having written the message Oliver wanted and included Robin's name in icing. Fondant flowers completed the design.

The cake sat on a stand in the kitchen where he worked on Neil's cake.

The kitchen was off–limits to customers, but he planned to hide the cakes when they were done.

Hearing customers come into the shop, he put his icing smoother aside and went through to serve them.

Sean parked his car outside the bakery and carried a box filled with jars of honey inside.

Two farmers were placing large orders for rolls, pancakes and pastries. Bradoch was bagging the items and piling them along the counter, working fast and efficient.

Seeing that Bradoch was busy, and that the counter was laden with orders, he thought he'd helpfully carry the honey delivery through to the kitchen. He'd done this before. The kitchen had never been off–limits to him.

'I'll pop these in the kitchen,' Sean called over to Bradoch, and started to head through.

'No, don't go in the kitchen!' Bradoch's panicked reaction took Sean aback. He stopped and wondered what was wrong.

'Just put the honey down on one of the tables,' said Bradoch, trying to sound less anxious. If Sean saw the two engagement cakes it could spark gossip.

'It's no bother to carry it through for you,' Sean told him, thinking maybe Bradoch was just over–stressed dealing with the customers.

'No, it's fine.' Bradoch's tone indicated the complete opposite.

Sensing something was amiss, Sean put the honey on one of the tables at the front window, gave Bradoch a friendly nod and then headed out, hearing the baker call after him.

'Thanks, Sean.'

The beemaster waved acknowledgement, got into his car and drove along to the sweet shop.

Muira was putting a jar of chocolate caramels up on a shelf, while Sylvia filled the display with macaroon bars, chocolate robins and toffee frying pans.

Sean came in with a tray of six jars of honey. He put it down on the counter and lifted Muira up, causing her to squeal and giggle. Lifting Muira up had become a regular bit of fun that they both enjoyed.

Muira would always scold Sean playfully, but she secretly loved this strong but gentle man, lifting her up in his capable arms.

'You're a scallywag,' Muira said, swiping at him.

Sean smiled down at her. 'I'm you're scallywag.'

He was indeed, Sylvia thought watching them, smiling to herself, seeing their relationship deepen.

Putting Muira gently down, Sean said, 'Do you know what's wrong with Bradoch?' He explained what had happened at the bakery.

'That's odd,' Muira agreed. 'He must've been hiding something in the kitchen.'

'I wonder what it is?' Sylvia couldn't imagine what could be so important.

Knightly was determined not to cause any drama, but the day was young.

He was well–dressed in dark trousers and an expensive white linen shirt. He'd attempted to tame the unruly strands of his rich, dark hair that had a tendency to fall over his forehead. On this, he scored an eight out of ten, but the day was young for that as well.

It was too early to have breakfast at nine with Amy at the castle. So having gleaned what cabin Laurie was staying in, from Walter when he delivered the groceries, he chapped on the door to visit his friend.

Laurie opened the door. In his early thirties, he was handsome, with a tall, lean, broad–shouldered build and pale grey eyes. His light brown hair was still damp from the shower, and he was dressed in jeans and a shirt, clean and tidy, ready to face the day. Just not prepared to be standing face–to–face with Knightly.

'When I booked this creative break in the heart of the Scottish Highlands, within a secluded castle's estate,' Knightly began. 'I didn't expect that my nearest neighbour would be twanging a guitar and tinkling a keyboard at all hours of the night.'

Laurie laughed. 'I don't twang my guitar. As I recall, you were the twanger.'

Knightly grinned. 'Playing guitar at that party we were last at wasn't my finest performance.'

Laurie pretended to disagree. 'It was strangely entertaining. I remember a few guests guffawing into their cocktails.'

Then they both laughed, and Laurie welcomed him in. 'Come on, I'll put the kettle on.'

Knightly stepped inside and looked around. 'Apart from the keyboard and guitars, your cabin is like mine.'

The windows offered a view of the lovely flowers and greenery and let in plenty of daylight. The decor was light and airy, white and cream with splashes of colour from the cushions and accessories. Luxurious and spacious, with a lounge, bedroom, kitchen and bathroom. Laurie had his musical instruments set up in the living room.

The cabins were dotted around the estate, and although technically Laurie was Knightly's nearest neighbour, their cabins were secluded and far enough apart to provide quietude and privacy.

Laurie started to make the tea. 'I love living here, though I've recently bought a house in the village. It's being renovated. I'm adding a recording studio so I don't have to keep travelling to the city to record my albums and tracks.'

'You're moving permanently from Edinburgh?'

'I am. I've extended my break at the cabin, and drive up to the city when I need to, but I'm making the village my home...with Sylvia.'

'I met her last night at the castle. She's a beautiful young woman.'

'And talented too.'

'She gave me a needle felted robin she'd made. My new lucky mascot. And apparently she enjoys quilting and makes delicious sweets.'

'Sylvia is a talented classical pianist,' Laurie revealed.

Knightly blinked. 'I noticed there's a baby grand piano in the castle's piano bar.'

'You should hear her play a concerto or rhapsody on that piano. She's played recently on a couple of my new tracks that are due to be released.'

'A hidden talent.'

'Muira, her aunt, knew she'd learned to play when she was a wee girl,' said Laurie. 'But none of the ladies in the crafting bee knew until Gaven bought the piano. I was on the Mullcairn radio show doing a live interview and phone–in. Etta and the other ladies were part of it, and that's when Sylvia's secret was revealed by Muira.'

'You heard about Sylvia's piano playing on the Mullcairn show?'

'That's where we first spoke. I met Sylvia, Etta, Jessy and the others live on the radio,' said Laurie. 'Then I met Sylvia when I arrived here the next day at the castle.'

'I've been warned that romance is flourishing at the village and that I should be careful not to fall in love.'

'I'd heed the warning if I were you. Unless you're looking for romance. In which case, you could be in luck.'

'Well, I do have my lucky mascot,' Knightly joked.

Laurie noticed the bag that Knightly was clutching as he handed him a cup of tea. 'What's in the bag?'

'My embroidery.'

Laurie smiled. 'The crafting bee ladies must love you.'

Knightly explained his predicament.

'I haven't met Amy, but Sylvia says she's an expert embroiderer, and here for the craft fair,' said Laurie.

'I'm meeting her for breakfast at the castle.' Knightly checked the time. 'Soon, so I'd better skedaddle. He drank his tea down and headed out.

'Enjoy your embroidery lesson,' Laurie told him. 'And be careful you don't fall for Amy.'

'I've no intention of doing so.'

Laurie gave him a look as if he wasn't convinced. 'You talk about Amy with a hint of...warmth in your voice. Though it's probably just you sounding dramatic.'

'Yes, totally not me being attracted to Amy. Even though she is lovely.'

They laughed, and Knightly walked away.

'Drop by any time you need to borrow a cup of sugar,' Laurie called after him.

'Thank you, neighbour.'

Their laughter filtered out into the morning air.

Knightly enjoyed the short stroll through the greenery, following a narrow path leading back to his cabin and onwards to the castle. Seeing the magnificent structure with the turrets rising up towards the light blue sky made him feel that maybe he should heed the warning. This was one of the most beautiful locations imaginable. And with the close–knit community welcoming him into their midst, he may well find it hard to leave.

'Your table for two is ready in the guests' dining room,' Walter said as Knightly walked into the reception. Walter was working behind the desk, along with Jessy.

'Amy's not here yet,' said Jessy. 'But away through and sit down. She'll not be long.'

Smiling, Knightly headed through to the dining room and a member of staff seated him at his table and handed him a menu.

The room was a mix of its historic past with floral cornices and original oil paintings, and the lightness of the present with modern elements in the decor.

Knightly was deciding whether to have the chef's special soufflé omelette with grilled tomatoes, mushrooms, beans and local pickle, or scrambled eggs and hot buttered toast, when Amy came walking in.

Wearing a pretty floral top, dark cords that suited her slender figure, and comfy black pumps, he thought she looked lovely. She'd brought her craft bag with her.

Several tables were filled with guests having breakfast, and Amy glanced around for a moment before seeing Knightly waving her over to their table.

Smiling at him, she walked across and he stood up to welcome her. Those eyes of hers looked at him, causing his heart to melt a little, a lot.

She sat down opposite him and he handed her the menu.

'I was thinking of having the chef's special omelette,' he said.

Amy glanced at the special on the menu and nodded. 'I'll join you. It sounds delicious.'

Ordering their breakfast, Knightly showed her he'd been working on the embroidery.

Amy blinked in surprise when he handed her the hoop. 'You've finished it. But I didn't show you how to whip the back stitches.'

'I caused a ruckus last night. Long story, better left untold,' he said. 'Anyway, I went back to my cabin and couldn't settle, so I started sewing. I finished the back stitches and then I checked up online how to do the whipped stitches. And voila!'

'Well done.' It wasn't perfect, but he'd learned the technique. 'You're now ready to learn satin stitch. I brought the acorn pattern with me. I'll show you after we've had breakfast.'

Knightly's smile lit up his handsome face and gorgeous blue eyes, causing her heart to react. She'd told herself that she wouldn't let herself fall for him at all. She was there to teach him embroidery. This wasn't a date.

'Where do you suggest I have my lesson?' he said.

'I thought your cabin, unless that's not suitable. We could use Jessy's cottage if you prefer.'

'My cabin is nearer. We'll go there after breakfast.'

CHAPTER EIGHT

Penny worked on her sewing and mending designs, repairing a vintage dress with creative embroidery. A delivery of vintage dresses and other pre–loved garments had arrived at her cottage recently, and she was working her way through the repairs each day and evening to finish them ready for the fair. And to take with her for her meeting in Edinburgh. A boutique was interested in buying the denim jackets she embellished with colourful embroidery thread, making the repairs design features.

Highlighting the repairs was something she loved doing, though she tended to use invisible mending on the dress hems.

One of the vintage dresses was made from midnight blue chiffon and the hem was torn. Penny had trimmed the damaged hem off and then created a new rolled hem and stitched it with her sewing machine. The dress was hanging on one of the rails in the spare bedroom that she used to store her stock. It sparkled with a glitter effect as if someone had worn it and run through stardust at midnight. She was reluctant to part with it, but this was a common issue as so many of the dresses and other garments felt like keepers.

She'd previously worked as a designer and pattern cutter for a fashion company in Glasgow, and still had contacts there, and clients in Edinburgh interested in her creative mending skills, even though she now worked from home, repairing beautiful clothes and making them wearable again.

Selling the garments on her website, she'd established her own business, and included videos of her various stitching techniques, showing her methods for mending a tear or worn fabric on jackets, dresses, skirts, jeans and tops. Her fashion experience and artistic talent combined to make the repairs a design feature of the garments. She'd been featured in magazines, and was becoming known in crafting circles for her visible mending — embroidering motifs such as the cornflower and bluebell she'd just finished stitching on to a denim jacket where it needed repaired.

Wearing jeans, repaired with colourful embroidery, and a white jumper she'd knitted, she padded around the living room in a pair of woollen socks she'd knitted herself. She loved knitting socks and jumpers. The socks would invariably become worn, and rather than discard them because of the work she'd put in to knitting them, she'd darn the holes with colourful yarn.

The front window of her living room overlooked the loch, and was on the same side as Neil's cottage. The back window offered a view of her garden and she liked to step outside and breathe in the fresh air while working hard.

Loving all sorts of crafts that involved sewing, from embroidery to quilting, she had a stash of fabric, thread, yarn and ribbons in a dresser in her living room, and a sewing machine set up, even though most of her repairs were hand sewn.

Morning sunlight streamed in the window, brightening her day, but the thought of having dinner with Neil later brightened it more.

Neil walked back to his cottage from the main street where he'd gone down to buy fresh groceries, including eggs for the Scotch pancakes, drop scones, he'd promised to make.

The light blue sky reflected off the loch, and with butterflies fluttering around the flowers and grass along the edges of the water, he could've been convinced it was a summer morning.

The temptation to pop in to see Penny crossed his mind, but he didn't want to interrupt her busy schedule. Things would quieten down soon, and their relationship was due to change to a whole new level, if she accepted his proposal.

He breathed deeply, calming his senses, not wanting to work himself up and become a worry wart.

Glancing along at her cottage, he went into his own garden, carrying his groceries, stepped inside and closed the door to the lovely day. He had work to tackle too. Less urgent than Penny's, but two wedding rings needed fashioned from yellow gold and white gold.

Sitting at his workbench, creating the rings under the overhead lights, he became lost in the lustre and design, loving his work, but still missing Penny.

Amy and Knightly walked through reception, heading out after having enjoyed their breakfast.

Gaven was behind the desk with Walter.

'Have you got a moment?' Gaven called to Amy and Knightly.

They went over to the desk.

'I've written a press release for the craft fair,' Gaven told them. 'I'm sending it out to the usual list of contacts, but I wondered if you'd have a look at it.'

They were happy to read it, and went through to Gaven's office behind reception and skim–read the press release on his computer screen.

'This seems interesting,' said Amy. 'The list of craft stalls is handy.'

Knightly read down some of the list. 'Knitting, quilting, embroidery, dressmaking, crochet, papercraft, needle felting, and rag doll making.' And then he read the summary about himself:

The well–known actor will be demonstrating how he embroiders acorns, a skill he's recently been learning from Amy, an embroidery expert.

Details of their names and links to their respective websites were included.

Come along and meet Knightly at the craft fair being held at the castle during the weekend.

Snacks and refreshments will be available in the marquees and in the castle.

Amy read about her embroidery demonstration, and felt a surge of nervous excitement.

Crafting demonstrations will be held throughout the fair. These include an embroidery demonstration from Amy. Knitting with Etta, Bee, Elspeth and Kity. Aileen's quilting. Penny's sewing and mending. And textile art techniques from Robin.

Amy and Knightly approved the press release.

'Great,' said Gaven. 'I'll get it sent off this morning. I'm attaching photos with it from last year's fair.'

'We're heading to my cabin for my embroidery lesson from Amy,' Knightly told him.

'Good luck,' said Gaven.

'He's already finished the lettering embroidery I gave him,' Amy told Gaven.

The laird smiled. 'Excellent.'

'I'm now about to attempt satin stitch,' Knightly explained.

And off they went, leaving Gaven to send the press release, and out into the sunny morning.

Amy and Knightly walked to his cabin. The sun flickered through the branches of the trees, casting glimmers of light along the grassy pathway from the castle, leading to where he was staying.

Knightly's cabin was nestled amid the trees, and a garden area surrounded it where marigolds, sunflowers and gerbera were flourishing. The whole atmosphere was inviting.

Knightly led Amy up to the front door, unlocked it and they stepped inside. He flicked a lamp on though it wasn't really necessary as the large windows let in lots of daylight.

Amy looked around the living room and nodded, impressed. 'I've never been inside any of the cabins, but I've seen pictures on the castle's website, and Jessy told me they were luxurious and comfy.'

'I'm delighted with it,' Knightly said, heading through to the kitchen. 'I'll make tea before we start. Feel free to nosy around.'

She did, noseying in the bedroom, loving the large window along the side of the bed. 'I'd feel like I was sleeping in the forest,' she called through to him, hearing him fill the kettle.

While the kettle boiled he came through to the bedroom and stood in the doorway, his height and broad shoulders filling it.

'Last night, I lay there gazing out the window. It's like how I imagine a fairytale forest would be with all the greenery and the night sky twinkling with stars.'

'That sounds amazing.' Her voice had a faraway tone, as if she was picturing how magical it would be. 'Jessy's cottage feels a bit like that. I fell asleep, lying in bed, gazing at the stars too.'

He looked at his bedroom. 'I'm sure it's equally relaxing during the day, if I get a chance to find out. I came here to unwind, but so far...'

'You've become involved in the craft fair. And with the crafting bee.'

He nodded. 'But I'd probably have found something to keep me busy.'

The kettle clicked off. 'I'll make the tea. Walter stocked me up with groceries.'

Amy looked around the living room. The felt robin was perched on a shelf. She tried to find any hints to Knightly's character. What would an actor bring with him for a break here? Authors, artists, musicians, she could picture their cabins would have books, a desk set up for writing or painting, and musical instruments.

But the actor's cabin revealed nothing about himself. The only thing she saw in the tidy living room was the remnants of thread where he'd been sitting on the couch working on his embroidery.

He carried the tea through and sat it down on a table.

'Where do we begin? Do I need to take the embroidered signature out of the hoop so we can refill it with the acorn pattern?'

Amy gave him a knowing look. 'You have been gleaning information online about embroidery, haven't you?'

'I noticed bits and pieces when I was researching the whipped back stitch,' he said.

Amy smiled. 'You're right, take the finished signature out of the hoop.'

She guided his hands, showing him how to remove the fabric from the hoop without damaging the embroidered signature.

Her hand accidentally brushed against his, and they both sensed the spark that charged between them.

Amy pulled her hand away first and pretended she hadn't felt anything.

Her silence caused him to keep his comments to himself. Secretly, he wondered if the attraction was going to cause ructions between them.

Amy put the finished embroidery aside, and gave him two pieces of white cotton fabric ready to be added to the hoop.

'Two pieces at the same time?' he said.

'Yes, I gave you a single piece for your signature embroidery, but for the type of pattern you're going to be working on, a backing fabric will keep your embroidery stable and help to hide any stray dark threads that could show through on a single layer of fabric.'

He studied the two pieces of white cotton material. 'Are they the same?'

'They are, but check the pieces and find the one without slubs on it. Little clumps of thread within the fabric, knotted bits. Look for the piece that is smoothest. We're going to use a pencil to draw the design on to the fabric.'

Knightly selected the smoothest.

Amy showed him how to correctly put the fabric in the hoop.

Then she took the acorn pattern out of her bag. The pattern was a dark illustration printed on white paper showing two small acorns and leaves. 'This is my acorn design.'

Knightly studied it. 'You drew this yourself?'

'Yes, I draw all my own patterns and designs. Some are more intricate than others. This design is easy to copy, drawing it by hand, on to the fabric ready for embroidering.'

Amy put the pattern down on the table, then placed the embroidery hoop on top with the fabric flush against the drawing. The outline of the pattern showed through.

'There are various ways to draw the pattern on. This is the method I use.'

Knightly nodded.

'Use light pencil lines to draw the outline of the acorns and leaves on to the fabric.' She showed him how to do this, keeping the pencil line thin and barely noticeable.

'The pattern lines will be covered by the embroidery thread, right?' he said.

Amy nodded and took the fabric out of the hoop, adding the second piece of fabric behind it, then put the two pieces together back into the hoop and secured the fabric tight.

'This creates a backing fabric for your embroidery,' she said.

Knightly nodded, picking up all the hints and tips.

'Now, I'll show you how to do satin stitch.' Amy dug into her bag and brought out two samples of the stitch on a bumblebee and a sunflower.

'I love this,' he said, running his fingers lightly over the surface of the bumblebee's body where each part was satin stitched in yellow, amber, white and black. 'I love bumbles. I'd like to embroider a bumblebee.'

'I'll teach you to do that. First, let's tackle the acorn embroidery. The whole design has only two stitches — satin stitch and whipped back stitch. You've already learned the whipped back stitch.'

Knightly looked more confident. 'So I only have to learn one more stitch — satin stitch.'

'That's correct.' She proceeded to show him how the stitches were sewn to create a smooth, satin–like finish.

Amy started the first few stitches on the bottom part of the acorn using two strands of rich, chocolate brown embroidery thread.

'I bring the needle up from the back of the fabric, right on the pencil line. Then I take the thread across the acorn and down through the opposite line. This creates a single, long stitch across the acorn. Now I repeat this, moving a fraction along the pattern line each time so that the acorn is filled in with smooth satin stitches.'

She handed him the hoop.

Knightly followed her lead. 'Is there a trick to keeping the stitches smooth? Mine aren't as tidy as yours.'

'It's just practise. Make sure the stitches lie flat and are close together.'

Knightly kept stitching, seeing the bottom part of the acorn filling up with the satin stitches.

He smiled at Amy. 'I'm getting the hang of this.'

'You pick things up really quickly.'

'Annoyingly so?'

'No, it'll make my job so much easier. You'll be able to demonstrate the acorn embroidery.' She was sure of this, seeing how adept Knightly was.

Sitting close together on the couch so she could guide his hands when necessary and help him change to a new thread, she felt herself react again to him. His hands were elegant, and every time they touched, a surge of excitement charged through her. She hoped he hadn't noticed.

'Sparks of energy,' he said, sensing the potent connection. 'We're making fast work on this design.'

Robin's morning was taken up with her textile art, creating the rich green colours of the forest and the atmosphere of the scenery she'd seen recently on her drive up to the castle.

Her strawberry–blonde hair was pinned up and she wore a pretty floral apron to shield her pink top and jeans.

She'd painted a large piece of white cotton fabric, like an artist's canvas, stretched tight across her work table, with shades of green, ranging from light, leafy tones and chartreuse to emerald.

The base of her textile art was now dry and she was adding pieces of white fabric, painted with watercolours in various greens, layering the work to create the textures of the forest.

Her cottage by the loch was her home and studio.

Art materials, her desk and sewing machine were along one wall in the living room. A chest of drawers was filled with the stash of fabric she used for her art, and a cream painted vintage dresser had shelves stacked with watercolour and acrylic paints, brushes, jars of beads, embroidery thread and crewel wool.

It was a fairly large living room with a wide window at the back looking out on to the garden and letting in lots of light. Some of her textile art paintings hung on the beige walls, adding colour to the decor.

Sketch books of her designs were open on a table.

She worked busily on the textured painting, adding layers to the design.

Once these layers were dry, she planned to add highlights of bronze, copper and gold tones to capture the autumnal quality of the forest that she'd felt when she was there. These would be created with pieces of painted fabric, including chiffon and other sheer material. She'd then embroider details using cotton and metallic effect thread.

While she worked, she wondered how Oliver's day was going. If she hadn't been so busy, she'd have popped down to the art shop to have lunch with him, as she often did.

She wiped her hands and messaged him:

Working through lunch. See you this evening. Love, Robin, x.

Okay, see you then. Love, Oliver, x.

Sylvia and Muira sat outside in the sweet shop's back garden having their lunch — Sylvia's homemade potato soup served with bread and a portion of salad. The soup was rich with potatoes, carrots, onion and spices.

Two trees arched over the bottom of the garden, creating a little arbour for garden seats and a table.

The shed was tucked at the side of the long lawn. Flowers grew in cultivated abandon around the edges of the garden and in pots where Sylvia had attempted to expand her gardening skills.

Sylvia loved sitting outside to have breakfast, lunch with Muira, or relax in the evenings after a busy day working in the shop. The sky always seemed vast overhead, making the garden feel bigger and a little bit magical in the evenings when the clear night skies were filled with stars. She'd recently added twinkle lights to the garden, but today, the sunlight had enticed them outside for a tasty lunch and a natter.

A notice on the front door read: *Open for sweetie emergencies. Knock loud.*

Oliver ran across from the art shop, read the notice and evaluated if his situated made the cut. Cupping his hand on the window, he peered in, past the jars of sweets, and saw that Sylvia and Muira weren't in the front shop.

Oliver knocked loudly on the door. And waited.

They heard the desperation in the knock, and having more or less finished their soup and salad, they gave each other a knowing look.

'Sweetie emergency,' Sylvia said calmly.

They'd yet to have a genuine one. Mild desperation for a bag of chocolate toffees or the notion for a macaroon bar were the usual measurements on the scale. Never a ten, or even a nine.

Muira nodded, and they headed through to find Oliver peering in the window.

'Four,' Sylvia estimated to Muira.

'Three and a half,' said Muira, and then unlocked the door to let Oliver in.

CHAPTER NINE

Knightly finished embroidering the small acorns and leaves, and smiled at Amy.

'What do you think for a first attempt at satin stitch?' he said, quite pleased with it. 'I don't need to be an expert. I'm only going to be demonstrating what I'm learning.'

Amy held the hoop and looked impressed yet again with his ability to pick things up quickly. 'Excellent. I think people will enjoy seeing you embroider this.'

'It's your design,' he credited her.

'And your embroidery.'

'What a team.'

His smile warmed her heart. They were still sitting together on the couch. The time had gone by in a hub of cheery chatter and creativity.

They enjoyed each other's company, and reluctant to call an end to this, Knightly suggested having lunch together. Amy took him up on his offer.

He went through to the kitchen and started opening the cupboards. 'What do you fancy? There are tins of soup — Scotch broth, lentil. I could do us beans on toast. I'm quite the expert on that culinary favourite.'

Amy checked the fridge for butter and found Scottish cheddar. 'Beans on cheesy toast?'

'Even better.'

Amy washed her hands and took charge of making the cheesy toast on thick slices of farmhouse bread. 'It's bubbling nicely under the grill, a bit of browning and we're done.'

'Beans at the ready,' said Knightly, heating them in a saucepan. He stirred them while preparing the mugs for the tea.

Grabbing two plates, Amy served up the cheesy toast.

Knightly poured the beans on top. 'Teamwork.'

He made the tea while she quickly added lettuce and sliced tomato on the side of their plates.

Working around each other, they orchestrated the snack lunch.

Before they sat down, Knightly peered out the kitchen window. 'Would you like to sit outside?'

'Oh, yes.'

There was a small wooden picnic table and chairs for two in the front garden.

Knightly laid napkins down on the table. Then they carried their plates and tea outside into the sunshine and sat down.

'Cheers,' he said, lifting up his mug.

Amy tipped her mug against his. 'Cheers.'

They continued to chat while they tucked into their lunch.

'I'd like to practise embroidering the acorn pattern,' he said.

'I'll give you a copy of the design and more thread and fabric that you can use.'

'Are you going to teach me how to embroider the bumblebee next? I know I'm not scheduled to demonstrate it, but I'd like to try making one.'

'I'd be happy to teach you. You should try using crewel wool to embroider the bee. It creates a soft texture to the bee's body, but I don't have any crewel wool with me. It's at Jessy's cottage.'

'We could go for a walk after lunch, and you could pick it up on the way,' he suggested.

'Okay. It's such a nice day.' She smiled and gazed around her. 'I was planning to take a walk through the estate while I'm staying here.'

'I explored part of it yesterday, but there's so much to see. I wouldn't mind the company.' He smiled warmly.

And she felt herself react again to him. Knightly was the unexpected acquaintance she'd made during her trip to stay with Jessy. Romance hadn't been part of her plan, only taking part in the craft fair and enjoying her embroidery. Now she was combining both, with the excitement of romance in the mix. She wasn't sure if she wanted this. She wasn't convinced that she didn't.

After finishing their lunch, they headed along to Jessy's cottage, not too far, but far enough to give them a pleasant stroll through the trees and greenery.

He insisted on carrying her craft bag for her.

'My bag has everything for embroidering, except crewel wool,' she scolded herself.

'This is far more fun than being prepared for every embroidery eventuality,' he assured her.

She nodded, agreeing with him.

Along the way, Knightly saw a niche with a shimmer of water shining in the sunlight. 'Is that a river or stream over there?'

Amy peered through the trees. 'I'm not sure, shall we take a slight detour?'

'I'm in the mood for adventure,' Knightly said in the dramatic tone she was becoming accustomed to hearing.

The adventurous pair walked over and as the greenery cleared, they found a stream running through part of the estate. They couldn't see where it started or ended as it tailed off in both directions into the trees and countryside.

Amy saw a small bridge arching over it and ventured on, eager to stand in the middle of it and gaze down at the stream trickling past.

Knightly stood beside her, blinking against the sparkling light as the clear water ran over the rocks on the bottom of the stream.

'Isn't this beautiful,' she said breathlessly. There was no one else around. No chatter of voices, only the light sound of birds chirping cheerily, a couple of bees buzzing in the lavender, and her heart beating with excitement.

'It is,' he agreed, but his focus was on Amy. She looked so lovely in the sunlight, smiling, enjoying this natural outdoor pleasure.

Amy cupped her hand to shield her eyes and peered across the stream. 'There's a swing over there. I want to have a go on it.'

Without waiting for him, she hurried over the bridge into the long grass and wildflowers where the two–seater swing hung securely between two sturdy trees.

Amy sat down on it, claiming it as hers. 'I used to love playing on the swings when I was a wee girl. I haven't been on one for years.'

'There's room for two,' he said, catching up. No subtle hint that he wanted to join her.

She budged up and he sat down.

'You've got the longest and strongest legs, so you kick off to get us going,' she urged him.

Laughing, Knightly started them swinging, then Amy helped build up the momentum until they were swinging with wild abandon on the long ropes that let them swing low and smooth and then high across the greenery.

Amy squealed as Knightly put on a burst of power, making them swing a bit higher. But she was loving every moment of it.

'This is wild,' he said, hearing his voice sound out into the clear air as they swung upwards into the blue sky.

'We're wild,' she told him. 'At least for today.'

'The day Amethyst and the actor went wild.'

For once, her full name didn't jar her. 'A day I'll always remember.'

Knightly knew it would be one he would treasure too.

Amy giggled. 'If Jessy and the ladies could see us now!'

'If the laird could see us now,' he added.

'If anyone could see us now,' she said with a sense of mischief.

'I won't tell if you won't.'

'Pinkie promise.'

With their free hands next to each other, they made a pinkie promise, and then still clasping Knightly's strong hand, she let him swing them higher up into the wide blue yonder.

'A box of chocolates,' Oliver said urgently to Muira and Sylvia when they wondered what he wanted. 'Luxury chocolates.'

He was waiting on a courier to arrive at his art shop to pick up an important delivery, and had run across to the sweet shop expecting it to have been open. And he knew that Robin was busy in her cottage, so she wouldn't see what he was up to. He wanted to surprise her.

'We have these boxes of popular chocolates that we buy in.' Muira pointed to the selection on a shelf.

'Or we can make up a box of our own special selection,' Sylvia told him.

'Are they for Robin?' said Muira.

'Yes. I want to surprise her with something nice this evening. And I just thought — chocolates.'

'Robin likes our chocolate truffles,' said Sylvia. 'And our chocolate toffee hearts, and chocolate dipped fudge.'

'Those sound perfect,' he said.

Sylvia showed him three sizes of boxes. 'I can make up a selection of lots of different chocolates. We have a special selection that includes one of each from our most popular flavours.'

Oliver nodded. 'Yes, do that. A large box please.'

'This box has two layers,' Sylvia explained, sitting the trays down on the counter. 'I'll put a dark chocolate, a milk and a white chocolate truffle in, a fudge square, a piece of Scottish tablet dipped in milk chocolate, a caramel cup, two chocolate hearts in milk and dark chocolate...'

Oliver watched as Sylvia filled the double layer box of chocolates, feeling sure that Robin would love this. He'd missed seeing her, and he wanted to surprise her with something a bit special when he saw her that evening.

Muira started making up the sweet orders that were due to be posted out later that afternoon, and the three of them chatted about the fair.

'Are you having one or two stalls?' he said.

'One,' said Muira. 'We'll both be there with our needle felting and knitting. And promoting our sweets.'

'The village is buzzing already,' he told them.

Muira bagged an order of nougat. 'I think it's going to be even more exciting than last year's fair, and it was popular.'

Sylvia finished filling the box, put the lid on and added a decorative bow. 'There you go, Oliver.'

'Thank you, and sorry for interrupting your lunch,' he apologised.

'That's okay, we'd finished it,' Sylvia assured him.

'And we're always open for sweetie emergencies,' Muira added with a smile.

Oliver smiled, but the tension in him was evident. They both sensed it, and exchanging a glance, Sylvia spoke up.

'Is everything okay, Oliver?'

He jolted. 'Yes, fine, why?'

Sylvia softened her tone. 'You just seem a wee bit...wound up.'

'Just work, and Robin's work, nothing else special, except the craft fair. We're both so busy.'

Muira nodded and smiled kindly. 'Gaven, Walter and Jessy organise everything at the castle's fair so that it runs smoothly.'

'Here, try a sample of my new marzipan sweets.' Sylvia offered him one from the tray of pumpkins, leaves and rosy apples. 'If you like marzipan.'

'I do, thanks.' He picked a pumpkin and popped it in his mouth. Then paid for the box of chocolates while chewing on the tasty treat.

'Do you know if Bradoch is up to something...secretive?' Sylvia said to him as she put the chocolate box in a paper bag and handed it to him.

'Bradoch? No, why?' Again, he jolted. Bradoch was up to a couple of secretive things — two engagement cakes. Had the gossip been sparked?

Muira explained. 'Sean says he delivered jars of honey to the bakery this morning. Bradoch was busy serving customers. But when Sean went to carry the honey through to the kitchen for him, Bradoch barred him from going through.'

'As if Bradoch was hiding something in the kitchen,' Sylvia added with a hint of suspicion.

The cakes! It had to be the engagement cakes. Oliver brushed their doubts aside. 'Nothing that I know of. Bradoch seemed fine when I saw him, cheery, not hiding anything. Nope. Nothing at all.'

Sylvia smiled tightly and exchanged a knowing glance with Muira.

Forcing a smile that everything was not suspicious, Oliver took his chocolates and left the shop.

Muira and Sylvia watched him through the window as he hurried over to his art shop and disappeared inside.

'They're definitely up to something,' said Sylvia.

Muira poured an assortment of chocolate peppermints into a bag, and agreed. 'We'll find out soon what it is. No secrets last long here.'

Oliver hid the box of chocolates upstairs, wished he'd bought a box of the marzipan sweets for himself, and then went back downstairs to finish a large watercolour he was working on.

He added details to the beautiful roses, sunflowers and marigolds, and the bumblebees buzzing around flowers. Painting always relaxed him, and he'd just started to feel less wound up when the courier arrived to pick up several of his paintings.

After the courier left, Oliver picked up his paint brush, then decided to message Bradoch:

The ladies suspect you're up to something. Sylvia and Muira just quizzed me in the sweet shop. They said you were acting secretive.

Sean nearly walked into the kitchen! I'd been icing the engagement cakes!

We need a plan.

Such as?

I don't know. I'm not the sneaky type.

Neither am I. Phone Neil.

Will do.

It was Neil's turn to jolt when Oliver phoned and told him their predicament.

'Tricky,' said Neil, pondering their options, unsure what to do. 'I'm not the sneaky type.'

'None of us are.'

Neil thought for a moment and came up with a suggestion. 'I'll phone Walter.'

'Yes, he'll know how we can wangle our way out of trouble,' said Oliver.

Neil phoned Walter at the castle and laid bare their problem.

'Leave it with me.' Walter kept his voice down. 'I'm working at the reception and Gaven's nearby. I'll phone you later. Tell Oliver and Bradoch to calm the beans.'

'Thanks, Walter.'

Neil finished the call and then phoned Oliver. 'Walter's on it. Tell Bradoch.'

After enjoying themselves on the swing, taking a wander through other parts of the estate, and sitting beside a natural pool that had a small waterfall and was shaded by the trees, Amy and Knightly eventually arrived at Jessy's cottage.

The sun had mellowed to a golden glow. They'd burned up the afternoon without even realising, having so much fun in each other's company, and enjoying the freedom to explore the expansive estate.

Amy unlocked the door and led the way inside. The day had darkened so much she flicked a couple of lamps on that shone a welcoming warmth in the living room.

Knightly looked around the quaint room. 'This is pretty.'

'It is,' Amy agreed, calling through from the kitchen while putting the kettle on for tea. They hadn't had a cuppa since lunch at his cabin, but the excursion outdoors was worth it.

A table at the side of one of the armchairs had a sewing basket set up, a lightbox, and a small pile of white cotton fabric, along with a large sweets tin now filled with embroidery thread.

Amy came through and opened up a biscuit tin packed with crewel wool.

'This is the crewel wool.'

'I like your tins.' He grinned at her.

'Any excuse to buy a tin of sweeties or biscuits,' she joked.

Knightly picked up two of the small skeins of crewel wool. 'This feels soft, like lightweight wool.'

Amy lifted a skein and pulled a length to show him. 'This crewel wool is 2 ply. It's used for crewel work embroidery. I love embroidering bees and birds with it because of the gorgeous colours and texture.'

'So it'll give a soft, woollen texture to my bumble.'

Amy laughed. 'It certainly will.' She lifted up three shades of yellow, from golden to amber. 'These are the colours I've used for my bumblebee pattern before along with the black and white.'

'Ideal for a bumblebee.'

The kettle clicked off. 'I'll make the tea and then we'll get started. Help yourself to a seven inch hoop, and there are pieces of white cotton fabric you can use. Pick one for the front of the embroidery and a piece for the backing. Put the top piece in the hoop.'

Leaving him to help himself, she went through to the kitchen and made two mugs of tea, then brought them through and sat them down on a separate table.

'I have a rule never to sit a mug of tea near my stash of embroidery threads,' she told him.

'I'll adhere to that, though I could do with a cuppa. It's been quite a day, and what an afternoon. But I won't tell.' He playfully held up a pinkie, reminding her of their light–hearted promise, and then went over and picked up a mug of tea.

Amy started to explain the process. 'It's the same as the acorn embroidery. You have to trace the embroidery pattern on to the top layer of fabric in the hoop. Then take it out, and put it back in the hoop with the backing fabric. Start stitching as you did before with the satin stitches and whipped back stitches.'

'So, we're just using a different type of thread. A woollen thread,' he said.

'Yes, it creates a lovely texture. The eyes and other small parts of the bee need only back stitches.'

'Okay.' He put his mug down out of the way, and showed her the fabric he'd put in the hoop. 'Is this correct so far?'

'Yes.' She got up and looked through her patterns and picked out the bumblebee design. 'Use the lightbox to trace the bee on to the fabric.' She switched it on and the whole surface lit up, shining the embroidery design clearly through the fabric.

'I can see why a lightbox is handy,' he said, sitting down and tracing the bee on to the fabric in the hoop.

'That's great,' she said, when he'd finished.

'Let me try to put the two layers of fabric in the hoop.' He'd seen how she'd done it, keeping the fabric smooth and tight.

'Well done. Now I'll show you how to thread a large–eye needle with the crewel wool, and how to start the embroidery by securing the thread at the back of the work.'

Knightly did as she instructed and then held the hoop ready to begin the satin stitches using one of the yellow tones of crewel wool. 'Is the stitch the same?'

'Yes, just follow the lines on the pattern. Bring the needle up through the fabric on one part of the bee's body, then down through the fabric, to fill each bit of the bee. Then repeat until each piece of the bee is filled in with the satin stitch. Check the picture on the pattern to see what colours to use.'

She watched as Knightly sat there learning how to embroider the bee.

There were moments again, as her hand brushed against his, that she felt such a spark of attraction. When they leaned close to talk about the embroidery, she could see into the depths of his gorgeous blue eyes.

Don't let your guard down, she warned herself. She was determined not to go home with a broken heart.

And yet...they seemed to get on so well together, liking the same things, enjoying being playful, never faltering for conversation.

As he took his time to sew each stitch as before, he talked about his plan to relax in the cabin.

'When I booked the break I planned to relax, read through a couple of scripts for plays I've been offered, and give my voice a rest.'

Amy laughed. 'And you haven't stopped talking since breakfast.'

'I've hardly stopped talking since I arrived!'

She smiled warmly at him.

'But it's been worth it. I've had so much fun, a bit of mischief with you, but that's our secret, and causing chaos last night outside the castle, but Walter sorted things out.'

Bradoch was dipping his doughnuts in sugar when he got a call from Walter.

'I'm going to phone Muira and tell her you were baking new recipe cakes for the autumn. The cakes were sitting in the kitchen being decorated. You didn't want anyone to see them, including Sean. Fair enough?'

'Yes, that should work. Cheers, Walter.'

'Nae bother. I'll call her now.'

Bradoch phoned Oliver to tell him Walter's plan.

Oliver told Neil.

Muira listened as Walter explained about the gossipmongering gone wrong. 'When it comes to his new cake recipes, Bradoch is a secret squirrel.'

'That explains things,' Muira agreed. 'Sylvia is like that with her new marzipan sweetie recipe.'

'Ach, I heard the gossip and spoke to Bradoch, and he said he's secretive about his new cakes,' said Walter. Not a complete lie.

'Thanks for telling us, Walter. I'll phone Sean.'

'I wonder what Bradoch's new cakes will be?' Sylvia sounded keen to know when Muira explained things to her.

'We'll buy them,' said Muira. 'Bradoch's cakes are always delicious.' Then she phoned Sean.

Sean was delighted to get a call from Muira, and relieved to know that nothing furtive was up with Bradoch. 'Are you busy tonight? Going to any crafting bees?'

'No, I've no plans.'

'Would you like to have dinner with me at my house? It'll just be the two of us. Campbell's going over to Bee's cottage.'

'That would be lovely. I'll come round after I've finished at the shop.' Muira beamed at Sylvia as she finished the call. 'I've got a dinner date with Sean.'

'Oooh! What are you going to wear?'

'What I've got on under my pinny. I'm going as soon as we lock up tonight.'

Sylvia shook her head. The blouse and skirt would never do. 'Rummage in my wardrobe and put something nice on.'

Muira's face lit up. 'Can I borrow that lovely floral blue tea dress?'

'Yes, and I've got the perfect lipstick you can wear with it.'

The two lamps that were on in the cottage as Amy continued to teach Knightly how to embroider a bumblebee, weren't enough to illuminate the living room as the sunlight faded.

Amy looked up. 'Where did the time go?'

'We've been busy bees,' he joked.

'It must be coming up teatime.'

Knightly stood up and eased the tension from his shoulders. 'I'll be on my way. But I'm taking my bumble with me to continue sewing the pattern.'

Seeing Knightly gather his things and head to the door, she made an impulsive offer. 'Do you want to stay for dinner? Mashed tatties and pie with gravy?'

Knightly reversed and came back in. 'I'll peel the tatties.'

Amy smiled. 'I'll put the pie in the oven. Jessy's freezer is well–stocked.'

Rolling his shirt sleeves up to reveal lean muscled forearms that set her senses alight, he followed her through to the kitchen.

Amy switched the oven on, planning to blame the heat if she got caught blushing. She really was trying not to let him affect her, but seeing his tall figure in the kitchen made her all the more sure that Knightly was a sheer temptation she'd need to try hard to resist.

He washed his hands at the sink and looked out the window at the garden and greenery beyond. The cottage had a homely feeling to it. Glancing at Amy busily preparing the pie, caused his heart to ache. He could act that he just wanted to be friends with her, but even with his years of theatrical experience, it was going to be difficult to hide how he felt about Amy.

CHAPTER TEN

Campbell came walking in from one of the fields, taking off his white beekeeping suit and hanging it up in the hallway of his father's house.

Sean was busy cooking dinner in the large, farmhouse–style kitchen. The aroma enticed Campbell to look in before having a quick shower and getting ready to head over to his girlfriend's cottage. Campbell had a tall, fit physique, burnished gold hair and gold–flecked green eyes.

When Campbell first arrived in the village recently, the crafting bee ladies initially thought he was a heartbreaker and a troublemaker. He hadn't broken Bee's heart, quite the opposite. They were happily dating, and although their romance was new, he knew their future was together. The troublemaking? Well, he tried not to cause it.

Sean used the quilted oven mitts, a gift from the crafting bee ladies, to pull the roasting tin out of the oven to check on the sizzling dinner.

'Roast tatties and roast parsnips,' Campbell said, peering over. 'Did I pick the wrong night not to be here?'

'Away and get ready for your date with Bee,' Sean told him. 'I'm cooking dinner for Muira. She'll be here after she locks up the sweet shop.' He checked the time. 'In about twenty minutes.'

Campbell smiled, happy for his father. 'Okay, I can take a hint.' Then he explained why he was taking his tool bag with him. 'Bee's spinning wheel has a wobble. I'm going over to sort her legs for her.'

Sean tried not to smirk. 'Have fun.'

'I will. Bee's cooking us dinner.' Though he still looked longingly at the roast.

'I've a big bag of tatties in the pantry, and plenty of vegetables, including parsnips. I'll rustle up a roast dinner for you another night,' Sean promised.

Campbell grinned, gave him the thumbs up, and hurried away.

Bee sat in her cottage kitchen, knitting a white lace shawl, while the dinner cooked.

An attractive amber blonde with blue eyes, she sold her knitwear and hand spun yarn from her website. Originally from the Shetlands, and then living in the Orkney islands too, she was able to move around easily with her knitting business.

She'd joined the local knitting and crafting bee nights, and after falling for Campbell, had decided to make the village her home.

A stew simmered away nicely on the stove.

The kitchen door was open, letting the fresh scent of the flowers from the back garden waft in.

Campbell wafted in with it, his hair still damp from the shower and wearing an open neck shirt and jeans. He wrapped his arms around her as she sat there, careful not to cause her to drop any stitches on the lace shawl she was knitting.

'Have I got time to sort your wobbly legs?' Campbell held up his tool bag.

'The stew will be ready in less than half an hour. Can you sort my wobble by then?'

They laughed, and he headed through to her knitting room, his words trailing behind him. 'Don't tempt me...'

Bee giggled, and as one of the most skilled knitters in the village, continued to knit at speed.

Amy and Knightly sat down at the kitchen table to have dinner.

'Something's bothering me,' he said, wanting this out of the way before they enjoyed the meal they'd cooked together.

Amy steeled herself.

'I can't keep taking your embroidery thread and fabric without reimbursing you. Teaching me shouldn't cost you.'

Amy let out a sigh of relief. 'I have plenty of fabric. You should see my stash at home. And the embroidery thread isn't expensive.'

'Yes, but I—'

'Thanks for being considerate of that, but it's fine,' she assured him.

Knightly smiled, but planned to make it up to her anyway. He didn't know how yet, but he'd figure something out.

'You look lovely,' Sylvia said to Muira, having insisted her aunt add a flick of mascara to her lashes, as well as using the flattering soft pink lipstick.

Muira smoothed her hands down the tea dress and smiled. 'Thanks, Sylvia. I hope you have a nice night with Laurie.'

Sylvia walked her through from the cottage accommodation at the back of the premises to the front of the shop and unlocked the door. 'Enjoy your dinner with Sean.'

'I wonder what he's made us tonight.'

'Something tasty no doubt.' Sylvia gave Muira an encouraging hug and then waved as Muira drove off to her dinner date. Then she jumped in the shower and got ready to head up to Laurie's cabin.

A short time later, Sylvia brushed her hair, put on her makeup, and wore a light blue dress, a thrifty buy from Penny, while listening to a popular radio show live from the studio in Edinburgh. The Mullcairn show.

Securing the sweet shop, Sylvia drove off, heading to the castle, tuning the car radio in. Listening to the show, she heard one of Laurie's popular songs being played. Sylvia sung along.

An amber sky stretched across the loch, making the water look like liquid gold in the early evening glow.

Lights were starting to shine from the cottages dotted around the loch. Sylvia saw a light on in Etta's cottage as she drove by and headed up to the forest road.

Etta sat in her living room, relaxing, knitting a Fair Isle jumper, and listening to her favourite radio presenter. Mullcairn was a mature man in his fifties, with a voice as smooth as malt whisky, and a mischievous sense of humour. He made Etta's heart beat faster every time she tuned in. She liked to listen to the radio when she was knitting. Mullcairn's show was her favourite, a mix of the latest news and music. She listened to his show all the time.

She'd once inadvertently taken part in one of his live phone–in chat shows, and spoke to Mullcairn himself. He'd ended up buying a Fair Isle jumper from her and she'd posted his order up to the studio in Edinburgh. Chatting to Mullcairn that evening was a memory she cherished.

Mullcairn's cheery voice sounded over the radio.

'*That was Laurie singing there. Those familiar with my show will remember Laurie being on as my guest recently. He told me was taking a creative break at a magnificent castle in the heart of the Highlands, owned by Gaven, the laird.*'

Etta perked up, stopped knitting, and listened intently.

'*A wee bit of news has come in this evening. There's an autumn craft fair being held at the castle soon. Check their website for details.*'

Etta scrambled to grab her phone and call Jessy at the castle.

'Jessy, Mullcairn's talking about the castle's autumn fair on the radio. Tune–in!'

'We are,' said Jessy, sounding excited. 'Walter has the radio on at reception. Gaven's listening too. He sent a press release to Mullcairn.'

Mullcairn continued. '*I'm hoping to swing by on the Sunday as the weekend fair has a ceilidh to round off the festivities. If you're listening, Gaven, I trust there's room at the castle for me. I'm bringing my kilt and sporran. I love a ceilidh.'*

Etta gasped. 'Mullcairn's coming to the castle!'

'Oooh, Etta. You'll get to dance with your heartthrob,' said Jessy.

'My heart's racing at the thought of it,' Etta confessed, fanning herself with a knitting pattern.

'So if you're attending the autumn craft fair,' Mullcairn added. *'And you see me meandering round the stalls, come over and say hello. Don't be shy. Do you hear that, Etta.'*

Etta clutched at her cardigan. 'Oh, I'm flabbergasted.'

Jessy squealed with delight. 'Mullcairn gave you a mention.'

Etta could hear Walter and Gaven's cheery reaction in the background.

'He remembers me,' said Etta.

'I'm not surprised. That was a wild night on the radio,' Jessy reminded her.

'Right,' Mullcairn concluded. *'Time for some wee jingles, followed by a new song from Brad, the popular American singer. Brad has opened a new recording studio in a small town north of New York. This was recorded there. It sounds great. A mix of pop and country to get you up dancing. But first, oor jingles.'*

The lively jingles started on cue.

Etta and Jessy spoke while the jingles played in the background.

'Gaven is phoning the studio right now, saying he's booked a room for Mullcairn as his guest at the castle,' Jessy told Etta.

Etta's heart fluttered. 'Oh, it's so exciting.'

Laurie was listening to Brad's new song on the radio as Sylvia arrived at his cabin.

He pulled her close, hugging and kissing the breath from her.

Sylvia was breathless too from the exciting news. 'Did you hear Mullcairn say he's coming to the craft fair?'

'Yes, that'll be a boost in publicity for the event. And I'll be pleased to meet him again.'

'I bet Etta is listening in. She'll be thrilled he mentioned her,' Sylvia said, starting to look through the kitchen for what they'd have for dinner.

'I've ordered dinner to be brought over from the castle. Chef's special. A little bit of everything delicious from the main menu,' he said.

'Great.' She listened to the song being played on the radio. 'I like Brad's new song.' She enjoyed his music, and had never heard this number before.

Laurie agreed, then he revealed a surprise. 'I know Brad. If he's opened a new recording studio, maybe I should give him a call and ask for any tips for the one I'm having built.'

'You know Brad?' Sylvia was still discovering so many things about Laurie's world.

'We met a few times on the tour circuits,' Laurie explained. 'He's genuinely nice, and talented. He writes his own music and plays and sings his own songs.'

Sylvia smiled at Laurie. 'So do you.'

Laurie pulled her close again, and was about to kiss her when Walter chapped on the cabin door. He'd brought their dinner, and was excited about Mullcairn coming to the castle.

'We were listening to the show,' said Laurie.

'It's great that the castle's fair got a mention.' Walter put their dinner down on the kitchen table. It was carefully packed.

The radio was still on. Jingles played in the background and then Mullcairn's voice filtered out, interrupting their conversation.

'I should mention that Knightly, the well–loved actor, is demonstrating his embroidery prowess at the craft fair. I can't knit or sew, but I'm going to have a peek at Knightly's embroidery. I believe he's stitching his acorns. The mind boggles.'

Oliver walked to Robin's cottage carrying the box of chocolates.

Twilight illuminated the loch, and as he headed along he pictured where he'd propose to Robin. Her garden merged with the greenery, dipping down to the edge of the loch where a sprinkling of flowers grew among the long wisps of grass, creating a pretty border around it.

He planned to invite her to go out for an evening stroll, after dinner, just the two of them. And there, by the loch, he'd ask Robin to be his wife. His stomach tightened at the thought that she'd want to postpone getting engaged until it suited both their busy schedules. He was prepared for that. Robin was far more sensible than him. But he wanted to throw sensibility to the wind.

At that moment, a breeze swept by him, causing him to gaze along towards the forest road ahead, and the castle turrets peeping over the trees against the vast starry sky.

Oliver took a deep breath. Not long now until the fair, a handful of days. So even less time to the night of the proposal. Two evenings before the fair.

He wished he could walk into the cottage tonight, and even without the ring in his pocket, propose to her, and end the doubt and trepidation. But he wanted to do it right. Make it special. A night to remember, when hopefully Robin accepted the engagement ring.

The cottage door was unlocked, and he went inside and through to the kitchen where he could smell the tasty aroma of dinner cooking.

'I made something easy,' Robin called to Oliver, hearing him coming in. 'Pasta.' She served up the cheese and tomato pasta with a sprinkling of grated cheese and parsley, and popped a few cherry tomatoes on top.

As she put the plates down on the kitchen table, she looked round at Oliver standing there holding the box of chocolates. She recognised the sweet shop box.

Robin blinked out of her industrious, culinary bubble. 'Chocolates.'

Oliver smiled at her.

She wiped her hands and walked over, opened the lid and looked at the delicious selection. 'These are a lot of my favourites.'

'Sylvia picked them.'

Robin's hand hovered over one of the dark chocolate truffles, and then resisted. 'I should have the pasta first.'

Oliver shrugged. 'Go wild, no rules tonight.'

She didn't need further persuasion and popped the truffle in her mouth, nodding, enjoying the rich chocolate flavour.

'What's the occasion?' she mumbled, wondering if she'd missed something.

'Nothing. Just you.'

On her tiptoes, she kissed him. A chocolate kiss, causing him to smile. The chocolates had been worthwhile.

'I'll put these through in the living room out of further temptation,' he said, carrying them away.

'Wise move, Oliver. Though that milk chocolate heart has my name on it.'

'The dark chocolate heart could tempt me,' he called through to her.

'What else could tempt you this evening?' Robin said, smiling as he came back into the kitchen.

'Seeing your new textile art designs,' he toyed with her. 'The progress you've made on the castle forest artwork.'

'I've left my work drying on the table. You can see it after dinner.'

Oliver pulled her into his arms. 'Though I think I'd much prefer more of those chocolate kisses.'

Robin played along. 'Handily, we've got a whole box to supply those.'

Smiling, they sat down to eat their pasta, chat about their day, and then planned to snuggle up in the living room having tea and chocolates.

Penny was running late, literally, running from her cottage along to Neil's cottage. She'd become caught up in sewing and mending a gorgeous vintage dress and hadn't realised the time.

Neil hadn't chased her up. No messages urging her to put a spurt on so he could make the pancakes as promised. His patience outmatched hers, she often admitted to herself.

Dashing in, she heard him call to her.

'I'm in the kitchen.'

Penny hurried through. 'Sorry, I lost track of the time.'

Neil smiled calmly and held up a jug. 'I've prepared the pancake mix. So relax, it's fine.'

He had the girdle on the stove, ready to cook the Scotch pancakes, the drop scones. The girdle was like a flat pan, and he'd bought it recently. The pancake mixture was made from flour, egg, milk and a couple of other ingredients, ready to be spooned on to the hot girdle, and cooked until light and golden.

Penny made the tea while Neil cooked two pancakes to get the process going. He put these, when cooked, on to a side plate. They were golden and delicious, just not perfect. The next lot would be.

Penny reached for one of them, armed with a fork. 'I want a raggy scone,' she insisted, but was careful as it was hot. She added a scraping of butter, watching it melt over the golden surface of the pancake.

Neil smiled, but liked that she was hungry and eager to enjoy the pancakes. Homely pleasures, with the woman he loved, meant more to him than all the gold nuggets in his safe.

But the diamond cluster engagement ring he had for her was burning a hole in the safe, or perhaps just in his thoughts, in his eagerness to propose. The timing wasn't right though. Look how busy Penny was right now. The special moment would be wrapped up in the whirlwind of work. The evening before the fair felt like the ideal time.

Brad's handsome face smiled out from Laurie's phone. The successful recording artist was around the same age and fit stature as Laurie, with sun lightened thick, blond hair and pale blue eyes.

Sylvia and Laurie had enjoyed their dinner in the cabin. Laurie had then called Brad. Sylvia was there listening.

'I had a former hardware store in the small town refurbished as a second recording studio. I have my main studio in New York, but I wanted away from the city to relax and find fresh inspiration for my song writing,' Brad explained.

'I'm hoping for something like that here in the Scottish village,' Laurie told him. 'What's the set–up in your new studio, if you don't mind sharing that with me.'

'Sure thing, Laurie. I have two main rooms for recording, a master control room, cutting edge equipment, and everything is kitted out to a professional standard. I used local builders to do the work.'

'I have local builders working on my property renovation too. I want the house to be homely, and the studio attached, but not intrusive, so I can get away from work, and enjoy my home life with Sylvia.'

Sylvia reacted to the permanent edge of Laurie's comment, but she was thrilled about this. She knew she loved him deeply, and that Laurie loved her too.

'Hey, there, Sylvia.' Brad waved to her and smiled.

'Hello, Brad. I love your music,' she told him, causing him to smile his thanks.

'I'm in the studio right now,' said Brad. 'Would you like a tour?'

'Yes, that would be great.' Laurie was eager to see it.

'Okay, this is the reception.' It was small but sleek. Two guitars and a saxophone hung on the walls, along with a framed poster of Brad playing his electric guitar. 'The main recording rooms are through here. There are two levels. The studio rooms are on the ground level, and I store equipment upstairs.'

Laurie and Sylvia watched as Brad continued along a narrow, carpeted hallway to the main control room. Windows were surplus to requirements. The studio was darker than Laurie had anticipated, but the spotlights created pockets of light that felt cosy and welcoming.

'The carpeting helps dampen the noise, and as I said, everything is sound–proofed,' Brad continued. 'This is the main control room with the recording equipment and mixing desk.' Brad gestured through two glass partitions. 'These are studio one and two where I perform. I invite others I know in the business to record sometimes as well. And that's about it, folks. Small, compact, but with the technical equipment, the multi–track mixing desks, microphones, and instruments, it's all I need. And all you probably need too, Laurie.'

A piano, keyboards and various guitars were seen in the background.

Laurie nodded, feeling he'd been planning the right type of studio. 'You've been so helpful, Brad. Cheers for that.'

'Sure, anytime you want to chat about your studio, call me.' Brad smiled and waved at them as the call came to a close.

Chatting about the fair and the studio, Sylvia and Laurie made tea in the kitchen, and both relaxed after their busy days.

'I saw this on the castle's website,' said Knightly, carrying a lantern from Jessy's cottage through the trees to the location nearby. 'It says it's a recent addition to the castle's estate that Gaven suggested.'

Amy was up for the night–time adventure after their dinner, and followed him along the grassy path to the clearing in the trees.

'Oh, this is magical.' Amy gasped.

They were surrounded by little solar twinkle lights draped through the trees.

'They remind me of dragonflies,' said Knightly.

'What a lovely idea.' Amy wished they could stay longer, but it was late in the evening and he'd suggested this on impulse. She'd been happy to go along, but obviously they couldn't linger here for too long.

Knightly took out his phone and beckoned her to stand next to him. 'Let's get a picture. People could think we're making this up.'

Amy tucked herself into Knightly, feeling an easy comfort in their closeness.

Knightly captured the moment and then showed her the picture.

And there they were, looking like a happy couple. For that evening they were, but Amy knew their futures lay in different worlds. But it was nice to dream a little, especially in a fairytale setting like this.

The adventure complete, Knightly walked Amy back to the cottage.

'Thank you for a wonderful day, and evening,' he said, holding a bag with the embroidery in it.

'I had fun.'

Promising that he'd keep practising his embroidery, Knightly waved and walked away to his cabin.

Amy stood at the door of the cottage watching the tall figure merge into the trees, and then she went inside. Jessy would be back soon, and she had a lot of gossip to tell her.

As Amy put the kettle on for a cup of tea, a message popped up on her phone:

I thought you'd like a copy. Knightly had sent the photo of the two of them standing together in the twinkle lights.

Yes, thank you. She planned to show Jessy and the other ladies.

Amy sensed that he wanted to say something else, and waited to see if another message came through. Nothing did.

In the glow of the nightlight shining through the bedroom window of his cabin, Knightly stripped off and got ready for bed. His thoughts were filled with Amy. He wished their circumstances were different, but soon she'd be leaving and going home to her small town. And he'd be at the cabin until his month's break was finished. Would their lives ever cross again, he wondered.

Sitting up in bed with the lights off, he scrolled through pictures of Amy's town on his phone, pondering his options. It looked quaint, though larger than the village.

Forcing himself to get some sleep, Knightly went to turn his phone off, along with the fanciful runaway thoughts about Amy and him. But there was a message for him:

I'd like to invite you to come on my radio show — the Mullcairn show, to talk about your embroidery demo at the castle's craft fair. We'll discuss your theatre work too, and what shows you're in for the winter and Christmas. It'll be a phone–in, so you can take part from your cabin or pop up to the studio if you prefer. I got your number from the laird. Hope you'll join me. Cheers, Mullcairn.

Knightly was familiar with Mullcairn and his show. His reply was an easy decision:

Happy to be on your show, Mullcairn. Great show. Send me the details. We'll chat soon. Knightly.

CHAPTER ELEVEN

The next morning, Amy had breakfast at the cottage with Jessy.

Jessy had made them porridge. Amy added fresh raspberries to hers and poured creamy milk on top.

They sat at the kitchen table catching up on all the news and gossip.

'Knightly's ability to learn embroidery is impressive,' said Amy. 'He wanted to embroider a bee using crewel wool.'

'He seems the type to throw himself wholeheartedly into things. And he certainly appears to be sweet on you.'

'There's nothing romantic going on,' Amy insisted, feeling this wasn't quite true. She'd sensed the spark between them. Under other circumstances maybe they would've taken things further and dated. But she'd be leaving soon.

Jessy sipped her tea and smiled. 'Well, at least you're having fun while you're here.'

Knightly sat in his cabin reading one of the scripts. He'd planned to take his time to decide which one he preferred. But now that he was due to be on the Mullcairn show, he needed to make a choice so he could talk about what play he'd be acting in.

He'd made himself tea and had just started to read the script for the Christmas drama he'd been offered, when Laurie knocked on his door.

Knightly opened it.

'I'm heading up to the castle for breakfast. Want to join me?' Laurie offered.

'Yes, I haven't had breakfast.' He was happy to take Laurie up on his offer and then come back and read the script.

They were walking away from the cabin when they heard a commotion going on ahead of them, hidden by the trees.

Knightly glanced at Laurie. 'It sounds like there's something happening.'

Walking on, they heard the men's voices shouting. 'Pull! Pull!'

Frowning at each other, they hurried to see what was going on, and found two large marquees being erected in readiness for the fair in the castle grounds.

'It looks like it's all hands on deck,' Knightly commented to Laurie.

Local builders were working hard to organise the tenting, assisted by every strong pair of hands that had turned up to help, including farmers. Gare, the farmer, was there accompanied by his brother, Fyn.

Campbell was helping to construct them. He'd trained as an architect, but had opted to be a beemaster, but he'd been hired by the laird to help design and build extra cabins for guests. And here he was, along with his father, Sean, using his experience to help put up the marquees. The plan was to erect the large tents, then this would enable the builders to lay the flooring, assemble the stalls, install the lighting, power and sound systems.

Oliver had turned up, along with Neil, and they were helping Walter to straighten the tarpaulin as it was hoisted.

Gaven was in the thick of it, dressed in his running gear. The fitted black T–shirt showed the laird's lean muscles, presenting another side to the usually sophisticated look of him. 'Pull!' Gaven shouted.

Knightly and Laurie nodded to each other and ran over to pitch in, grabbing the ropes and adding their weight and strength to the endeavour.

'Pull! Pull!' Knightly shouted, using his powerful theatrical voice to spur them on.

Gaven nodded across to them. A look of thanks that they were willing to help.

'Pull!' Knightly and Gaven shouted in unison, helping to urge the men on, as the marquees started to rise and become fully erect.

The builders and others ran to secure them in place while the rest of the men held the marquees steady.

Finally, the marquees were solidly up and looking ready for the interior work to be done next.

The volunteers smiled, cheered themselves and laughed together, but as they went to leave, Gaven insisted they have a hearty breakfast that had been laid on by chef and the staff. What looked like gallons of tea was being poured into mugs on a large buffet table nearby in the autumn sunshine. There were plates piled with buttered toast, and fresh baked morning rolls filled with Lorne sausage, slices of square sausage, cheese or eggs. Lashings of beans, tomato and brown sauce were offered.

The men tucked in, and Knightly and Laurie joined them. It was breakfast at the castle, just a bit different than they'd planned, but they'd enjoyed being part of the community's efforts.

Bee phoned Etta at her cottage. 'I've just been talking to Elspeth on the phone. She's going to send a large bundle of her yarn to me ahead of coming here for the fair. I'll store the delivery in my cottage.'

'That's a great idea,' said Etta.

'Elspeth plans to load up her car and drive over from the island on the ferry. But this will let her sell extra yarn at her stall,' Bee explained. 'I wondered if you should suggest the same to Kity. I'll store Kity's yarn at my cottage too.'

'I'll phone Kity right now,' said Etta. 'Thanks for the suggestion. And are you sure you want to store Kity's yarn? I could find space for it at my cottage.'

'I've plenty of room to store it,' Bee insisted. 'Tell Kity to post the delivery to me.'

'Thanks, Bee.'

'And I was thinking of having a wee get together for the crafting bee ladies at my cottage a couple of nights before the fair,' said Bee. 'We can help each other with last minute things needing done, and have a natter. Bring your knitting.'

'I will, and I'll bring a cake.'

After chatting to Etta, Bee phoned several of the other members, and all of them were delighted to accept, including Robin.

'Two nights before the fair, yes, I'd be happy to come along,' Robin told Bee. 'I thought it would be nice to get together then, as we're bound to be busy the evening before the fair.'

'Yes, and I don't have anything special planned that night,' said Robin.

'No, it's two nights before the fair!' Oliver's reaction took Robin aback.

They were having their dinner at Robin's cottage when she'd told him about Bee's invitation.

She stared in surprise at him across the kitchen table. 'What's wrong with that? It's not as if it's the evening before the fair when I'll be fiddling with last minute things and then trying to get an early night.'

Oliver put his cutlery down. He'd lost his appetite for his crinkle chips. What was he going to say? Robin was looking right at him. She'd suss if he was lying. He took a deep breath. The only way out of this pickle was to tell the truth. Just not the true version of it.

Suitably confusing himself, Oliver began. 'The truth is...I was hoping that we could have a cosy night together. Just you and me. An evening without work or anything like that. It's been a crazy busy time, and sometimes recently...we've hardly had any full spare evenings to be together.'

The sincerity in his eyes melted her heart. 'Okay, I'll tell Bee I'm having the night with you,' she said calmly. There would be plenty of other crafting bee nights.

Oliver breathed a sigh of relief.

Robin smiled over at him. 'Eat your dinner, and tell me about your day.' She'd told him about hers while cooking dinner, that she was snowed under with work, for customer orders, and for the textile art she wanted to display at the fair. They were having dinner, but then the plan was for Oliver to leave and let her continue working that evening. That plan was still in place, and emphasised Oliver's wish for a relaxing night in together.

His day?...

He'd looked at her engagement ring a few times. He'd hidden the velvet ring box upstairs in his accommodation above the art shop, in a dresser drawer, right at the back, jammed in behind a folded jumper where it was safe.

He'd sketched the ring, aiming to present Robin with a framed watercolour of it as part of her engagement gifts. He was going to paint it later that evening when he went back to the art shop.

Another gift was ordered in advance from Fyn's flower shop. A bouquet of her favourite flowers. He told Fyn he'd pick it up two days before the fair. Fyn didn't pry if there was a special occasion. Oliver's secretive attitude curtailed that.

His expensive and elegant dark suit was back from the cleaners, pressed and hanging in his wardrobe along with a white shirt and silk tie. Shoes were polished and in the bottom of the wardrobe. He'd be dressed to impress when he proposed.

This evening, he wore his usual neutral casuals, tidy but not overdressed.

He'd toyed with the idea of having his dark brown hair cut, but decided not to mess with it. If the trim went awry, he wouldn't have time to grow it out. His hair was fine. He'd slick it back if necessary.

Bradoch baked delicious savoury pies with shortcrust pastry. He'd bought two. One as backup. He'd brought these with him that evening and popped them in Robin's freezer, saying how handy they'd be on other nights when they didn't want to fuss cooking dinner. Like the proposal night. He'd added luxury store cupboard groceries, and put them in her kitchen, telling her he'd ordered more than he needed, and again they'd be tasty with the pies. Robin didn't suspect his skulduggery.

His day had been a whirlwind of proposal preparations.

'Just painting,' said Oliver, and picked up his fork.

The following day, Knightly chose to go to the studio in Edinburgh to take part in the Mullcairn show. Studios, theatres, he was comfortable in those, so rather than participate in the live chat from his cabin, he'd driven to the city.

Doubling up on his visit, he'd dropped by to talk to one of the theatre directors he was due to work with, accepting the part in the Christmas drama he'd been offered. He loved the script, the lead character in the classic play, and the weekend only performances suited him. Leaving the weekdays free, enabled him to make other plans.

He'd set off from his cabin in the morning, had lunch at the theatre with the director, checked in on his house in Edinburgh, feeling the usual unfamiliarity of his own home when he'd been away, but this time...it felt less homely than ever. As if he was wearying for something that the house couldn't ever provide. Or someone to share it with.

Amy shot into his thoughts, and through his heart. Despite heeding the warning not to fall in love in the village, his efforts had been thwarted. He cared for her deeply, and it would be so easy to let himself go all the way.

Spending no more than a cursory stop in his house, checking everything was secure, he locked up and left without a backwards glance. His thoughts were on the forthcoming interview with Mullcairn. And wondering if Amy would be listening in. He intended taking her by surprise, naming her, and giving her the credit for his newfound embroidery skills.

Knightly had been to the studios before, as a guest on other shows, but never on Mullcairn's show.

An assistant welcomed him and showed him through to the studio where an even warmer welcome was given to him by Mullcairn.

'Thanks for driving up here, Knightly. Great to meet you in person. I've seen you perform on stage. I was at a Christmas show you were acting in last year. I fair enjoyed it.'

'I'm just hot from a meeting with that theatre's director. I've accepted the lead part in their new Christmas drama this year.'

'Great stuff. We'll chat about that in a jiffy. Let's get you seated and mic'd up.'

Headphones were placed on Knightly's head by a studio assistant. His microphone was tested for clarity and volume, and within a few minutes they were ready to roll.

Jingles played in the background, followed by a popular song, as they got ready to start the live chat. The show had already been going. Now the live interview part of the show was being introduced.

'I'll introduce you, then we'll dive right into the interview. Okay?' Mullcairn said to Knightly.

'Yes,' Knightly confirmed.

Mullcairn gave a thumbs up through the large glass window that separated his studio from one of the control engineers.

An *on air in two minutes* sign lit up.

Knightly calmly watched the time tick down. It reminded him of the start of the stage plays when the audience settled in their seats, the lights dimmed, the music or atmospheric sounds started, and then, on cue, he'd walk on stage.

Two seconds to go.

Mullcairn nodded to Knightly and smiled reassuringly. He didn't need to tell a seasoned performer like him what to do to engage the listeners.

As the song finished, Mullcairn's cheery voice began.

'*Well–loved actor, Knightly, has just arrived in the studio. He's looking fit and relaxed, so I'm assuming his creative break at the laird's castle is agreeing with him. Good evening, Knightly.*'

'*Good evening, Mullcairn.*' Knightly's rich tone sounded well over the radio...

Amy was at the castle, listening to the show at reception along with Jessy, Walter and Gaven.

Others throughout the village, including Etta, knitting in her cottage, were tuned in, while working at home on their crafts for the fair.

'*The break at the castle has bolstered me,*' Knightly agreed. '*It's a luxurious cabin set in beautiful countryside near the castle. Gaven, the laird, has been welcoming, as have the staff, like Walter and Jessy.*'

Jessy, Walter and Gaven smiled at the mention of their names.

'*But I have to say, it's been the welcome from the people in the local community that has heartened me more than anything. Especially the ladies of the crafting bee.*'

'*Ah, would that be Etta, Aileen, Muira and Sylvia?*' Mullcairn listed them off, showing his familiarity with them.

'*It would. And a young lady called Amethyst, known as Amy. An expert at embroidery. She's Jessy's niece, and she's staying at Jessy's cottage on the castle's estate to take part in the autumn craft fair.*'

'*Hello, Amethyst. Amy. I hope you're listening to the show,*' Mullcairn said chirpily.

Amy gasped when she heard Mullcairn mention her.

'*I need to give Amy the credit for teaching me how to embroider,*' Knightly announced.

'*I hear you're demonstrating your embroidery skills at the craft fair. Embroidering your acorns.*'

Knightly laughed. '*I am. And maybe a few wee extras. Amy has taught me to whip stitch my name, my signature. And how to embroider a bumblebee using crewel wool. Something I'd never heard of before I met the crafting bee ladies.'*

'*Acorns and your bumble! Do you hear that folks? Worth popping along to the fair to see that,*' Mullcairn joked.

The interview continued on a cheery wave of information about the stalls at the fair and the castle.

Mullcairn introduced the live chat. '*We're going to hear a song now. But stay tuned. We're opening up the phone lines for a live chat. If you have a burning question for Knightly, call the number that'll be given in a moment.*'

Mullcairn and Knightly chatted candidly while they were off air during the song.

'So you really have learned embroidery,' said Mullcairn.

'Yes, I never intended to, but...' Knightly shrugged.

Mullcairn laughed. 'I'm thinking the crafting bee ladies are a force to be reckoned with. In a nice way.'

'They are. And I've heard that your dance card for the ceilidh is filling up,' Knightly joked with him.

'Is Etta's name on it?'

'Top of the list.'

Mullcairn laughed.

Amy's cheeks were rosy. Jessy smiled at her. 'Knightly certainly comes across as being enamoured with you.'

He did. Never mind any burning questions, her cheeks were burning from hearing Knightly talk about her on the radio.

'I didn't know that Knightly had extended his repertoire.' Gaven looked pleased. 'A woolly bumblebee? And his signature. Well done, Amy. You've taught Knightly to really give a great demonstration. I'll be sure to add this to the website.' Gaven hurried through to update the website in his office behind reception, while still being able to listen to the show.

'*We have a first caller,*' Mullcairn announced. '*What would you like to ask Knightly?*'

And the questions began, with Knightly deftly answering them entertainingly. They were mainly about his acting roles.

'*I believe you've accepted the lead role in a new Christmas drama this year,*' said Mullcairn.

'*Yes, I spoke to the theatre director today, just before I came to the studio,*' Knightly named the theatre in Edinburgh where the show was scheduled.

'*Can you reveal anything about the role? Or is it a secret at the moment?*' said Mullcairn.

'*It's a classic festive drama, set in Edinburgh of yesteryear, lots of snow, atmospheric,*' Knightly revealed. '*I love the script. There's everything from a rammy to romance. I'll enjoy portraying a stooshie on stage. And I like the element of romance threaded throughout the storyline.*'

'*A rumpus and romance. It sounds entertaining. I'll be buying a front row seat for that performance. And what about any romance in your real life?*' Mullcairn prompted him.

'*Tricky one.*'

'*Romance always is,*' Mullcairn agreed.

CHAPTER TWELVE

Amy held her breath. Would Knightly reveal his true feelings? Did he have any romantic feelings for her? Or was she mistaking friendship for something more?

'*I'm not dating anyone at the moment,*' Knightly announced over the radio. '*But I'm keeping an open mind, and an open heart.*'

'*Dangerous territory,*' Mullcairn warned him.

'*It is. And this is the first time I've kept my guard down in a while. But I'd like to find the woman for me and settle down.*'

'*I've heard that romance is rife in the village. Perhaps you'll find her there.*'

'*Maybe I will. And I'd caution you when you come to the craft fair and the ceilidh not to fall for any of the local ladies.*'

Mullcairn laughed. '*My dance card is marked, so you never know.*'

A musical interlude curtailed their conversation, with Mullcairn introducing a song.

'*This is one of Laurie's lively songs. He was a guest on the show recently, and he's another talented entertainer to enjoy the hospitality of the laird's castle.*' Mullcairn lowered his voice jokingly. '*In case he's listening in, which I doubt, I'll let you into a wee secret. I've heard he's dating a lovely young lady from the village. I won't name her, but she plays the piano beautifully.*'

And then Laurie's guitar was heard playing the open riff of his song.

Mullcairn chatted to Knightly off–air while the song played. 'Have you met Laurie yet at the castle?'

'I have. I know Laurie. We tried to have breakfast at the castle yesterday but...' Knightly explained the marquee melee.

'For a buttered piece filled with a slice Lorne sausage, and a mug of tea, in the fresh air at the castle, I'd have pitched in as well,' said Mullcairn.

Knightly smiled. 'I had a workout, and a scrambled egg roll.'

Mullcairn looked thoughtful. 'I wonder if any of the crafting bee ladies will phone into the show tonight?'

'Like Etta?' said Knightly.

'Aye, Etta. She says she listens to all my shows.'

'I'm sensing you've got a fancy for oor Etta.'

Mullcairn didn't deny it. 'You've met her. What's she like?'

'A wee gem. I warmed to her right away.'

'I liked her attitude. She made me smile.'

'With Etta, what you see is what you get. She's been kind to me since I met her.'

Mullcairn nodded thoughtfully...

Aileen knocked on Etta's cottage door.

Etta hurried through to open it.

'Are you going to phone the live chat with Mullcairn?' said Aileen, arriving with her craft bag full of cotton fabric scraps for making a hexie quilt.

'No, but I was listening to Knightly.' Etta led Aileen through to the living room and they sat down near the radio.

'Knightly comes across well,' said Aileen.

'He does, and he's got a gorgeous voice. So has Mullcairn.'

'What are you going to wear to the ceilidh when you dance with your heartthrob?'

'Mullcairn could be mobbed with admirers. I might not get a look in.'

'Och, you will so. Mullcairn will make sure he dances with you. He even said as much on the radio.'

Etta adjusted her cardigan. 'I'll probably have a browse through Penny's new vintage dresses. She said she had lots of new dresses arrive.'

'*Right*,' Mullcairn said after Laurie's song. '*I hope you've been up jigging to that lively tune. We have here in the studio.*' Mullcairn winked jokingly to Knightly. '*But now you can all sit down and join in the chat again. Got a question for Knightly, or me? Phone in. You know our number.*'

A studio assistant signalled to Mullcairn through the glass partition and made an urgent winding motion with their hands.

Mullcairn got the message. '*So while you think up a question, here are some wee jingles.*'

The assistant spoke through to Mullcairn. 'Laurie is on the line.'

'Cheery or carnaptious?' Mullcairn wondered if Laurie was livid with him for revealing his romance with Sylvia.

'Seems cheery, and wants to chat to you.'

'Put him through. If we end up gabbing, stick another jingle on,' said Mullcairn.

'Will do,' said the assistant.

'Just a quick call,' Laurie said to Mullcairn. 'I want to thank you for playing my songs on your show.'

'Your songs are popular with our listeners,' said Mullcairn. 'But thanks for calling.'

'And Sylvia's still blushing, but delighted with your comments,' Laurie added.

Mullcairn laughed. 'Are you interested in joining us on the show?'

'No, it's Knightly's evening. I'm enjoying listening in,' said Laurie.

'Okay, but before you go, what are you up to? Anything newsworthy I should know about, or mention?'

'I'm building my own recording studio in the village. Refurbishing a house to include a studio. I spoke to Brad. You played one of his songs recently. And he's given me a few tips. He's built a music studio in a small town up from New York.'

'Interesting. I'll need to have you on the show to talk about your new studio when it's ready,' Mullcairn insisted.

'I'll be happy to do that.'

'And is there any chance you could have Brad call me? I'd love to interview him on the show.'

'Yes, I'll phone him and give him your number,' Laurie promised.

'Cheers, Laurie.'

The jingles were coming to a close. 'I'll away and let you get on with interviewing Knightly.'

'We'll have you on the show again soon,' said Mullcairn.

The jingles finished.

'*And we're back with our live chat,*' Mullcairn announced. '*Knightly was telling me that he helped put up the marquees for the craft fair. And Laurie was pitching in as well. Now that's what I call getting involved in an event.*'

'*The laird laid on breakfast afterwards,*' said Knightly.

'*Gaven sounds like a fine laird.*'

'*He is, and takes his responsibility as the laird to heart. He's working hard to make the craft fair a success.*'

'*I'm sure it will be. Tell me, will you be demonstrating your embroidery at one of the stalls? Can folk chat to you there?*'

'*I'll be on stage, showing my embroidery. People are welcome to come up and chat.*'

'*What about Amy? Will she be at the fair?*'

'*Yes, Amy will have an embroidery stall there. She'll be demonstrating her embroidery techniques. A few of the crafting bee ladies are giving demonstrations at their stalls. Etta is knitting. Aileen is quilting. All the details are on the castle's website.*'

Gaven smiled at Jessy and Amy. 'Knightly's doing a great job of promoting the fair.'

Walter was looking at the bookings on the castle's website. 'This could be our busiest craft fair.' He read the updated list of things Knightly was due to demonstrate on stage. 'Oh, did Knightly confirm he's giving a display of Highland dancing?'

Gaven blinked. 'You told me he was doing it.'

Walter bit his lip. 'Crossed wires. I said there was a rumour that he'd do a Highland Fling.'

'I've announced he's performing it on stage at the fair,' said Gaven. 'I'll edit the updates on the website before anyone notices.'

As Gaven hurried through to his office to do this, they heard Mullcairn announce on the radio...

'*I've just had a peek at the latest news on the castle's website. Apart from showing us your embroidery, I notice you'll be treating us to a Highland Fling.*'

Knightly tried to smile. '*Is that what it says on the website?*'

'*Yes, was that supposed to be a special surprise?*'

It was a surprise to Knightly. '*My grand finale,*' he lied, not wanting to dash anyone's hopes now that this had been announced live on air. With a bit of luck, the weights were still tucked into his sporran.

Neil turned the radio off when the Mullcairn show finished. He'd been sitting in his living room listening to the show with Penny after they'd had dinner.

'That was an entertaining show with Knightly and Mullcairn,' said Penny.

'It was,' Neil agreed, and then went through to the kitchen to make them a cup of tea.

Penny stretched and stood up from where she'd been sitting comfy on the couch with Neil, and followed him through. While he filled the kettle, she opened the back door to breathe in the evening air.

But as she went to step outside into the garden Neil secretly panicked that she'd see the unlit twinkle lights entwined through the flowers.

Hurrying over, he clasped her hand, pulled her gently into his arms, and all but lifted her back into the kitchen.

Penny giggled. 'Someone is in a playful mood this evening.'

Neil nudged the kitchen door shut. 'Don't let the cold air in. It's nice and cosy in here. Let's drink our tea and coorie in again before you have to go.'

Penny had said she'd planned an early start to her morning, sewing several items of clothing, getting them ready for customers and for the fair.

She smiled, happy with his suggestion.

Neil made the tea and they took their cups through to the living room to snuggle and chat before she left.

'Bee's having a crafting night at her cottage,' Penny told him. 'Most of the ladies are going along. I thought I'd go too. We're helping each other with last minute things for the fair. I'll take some of the dresses along as a few of the ladies are interested in trying them on. Everyone's planning what to wear to the ceilidh dance.'

Neil smiled at her. 'I'm looking forward to dancing with you.'

'I'd better wear something wonderful then,' she said lightly.

'You always look wonderful to me.'

Penny snuggled into Neil, and they chatted until it was time for her to leave.

Amy lay in bed rewinding the radio interview, going over Knightly's comments about romance and wanting to find the woman for him and settle down.

Brushing aside fanciful thoughts that maybe, just maybe, she could be that woman, she snuggled down to get some sleep. It had been a long and busy day, but she'd got a fair bit of embroidery work done, even though the evening was taken up listening to the Mullcairn show with Jessy and the others at the castle.

Gaven had admitted he'd need to check with Knightly about the Highland Fling performance.

As she lay there, a message sounded from her phone on the bedside table. She checked the message:

I hope you heard the show. I had a great time with Mullcairn. I'm driving back from Edinburgh now. Knightly.

Smiling to herself that he'd messaged her, Amy snuggled down again and fell asleep.

'It's fine,' Knightly assured Gaven the following morning. Knightly had gone to the castle for breakfast and the laird came over to talk to him. 'I'll do the Highland Fling.'

'I thought you'd agreed to do it. That's why I announced it on the website.' Gaven explained.

'I've got my kilt with me, so I'll give it a burl on the stage. I'm not going commando in case you're wondering. So make sure to tell everyone if they think otherwise.'

Gaven smiled. 'I will. Thanks again for going along with this. And for the great way you spoke about the castle's fair on the show.'

'It's a win for all of us. And even Laurie phoned up to talk for a minute to Mullcairn.'

'Walter says Laurie won't be here for the fair as he's away performing that weekend.'

'Yes, but he's hoping to arrive back in time for the ceilidh on the Sunday night.'

'Excellent.'

Gaven left and went back through to reception as Knightly's breakfast was served. Another of chef's specials to set him up for the day. He planned to practise a bit of embroidery, then dust off his kilt and dance around in his cabin, privately reacquainting himself with the Highland Fling. As it was danced more or less on the spot, he didn't need a lot of room to rehearse the fling he'd performed many a night on stage. He was sure it would all come back to him.

And it did. Later, in the seclusion of his cabin, he put on some Scottish music, and wearing his kilt, ghillie shirt, ceilidh dance shoes and sporran, he found that he remembered the dance as if it was yesterday.

A seasoned performer, this would be the easy part of his performances at the fair on the Saturday and Sunday afternoons he'd agreed with Gaven. The hard part would be the embroidery, but he'd learned enough to show his skills, and he'd had a great teacher in Amy.

He'd thought about inviting her to have breakfast with him that morning, then decided she'd surely need time to work on her embroidery. He'd already encroached on a lot of her time.

In the late afternoon, Knightly put his walking boots on and ventured out to explore the estate and surrounding area down by the loch. Eventually, he found himself outside the sweet shop, and seeing the tasty selection of sweets in the window, he couldn't resist going inside to buy some.

Sylvia and Muira were busy refilling jars and tidying up. The day was almost over and they were due to lock up soon and get ready for their craft night at Bee's cottage.

But they were happy to see Knightly and smiled as he walked in and looked around at all the sweets.

'I'm in to be tempted,' said Knightly.

Sylvia grinned. 'I knew you couldn't resist for long.'

'What kind of sweeties would you like?' Muira gestured around her.

'I'm open to suggestions,' he said.

Clearly this was the right thing to say to Sylvia and Muira, and they began selecting popular sweets, everything from chocolates to Scottish tablet.

Knightly accepted a sample of Sylvia's marzipan and popped a pumpkin in his mouth, nodding as he enjoyed the flavour. 'Delicious.'

'Would you like treacle toffee and a few bon bons?' Sylvia offered.

'Oh, yes,' he said.

'I'd recommend the nougat,' Muira suggested.

Knightly accepted the selection they offered him. 'These will keep me going for a week.' Picking up the large bag of sweets he'd bought, he smiled and left the shop. Sylvia waved him off, and turned the sign on the shop to closed before locking the door.

The other shops in the main street were getting ready to close for the day too.

Knightly had only just stepped outside the sweet shop when he saw Oliver dash out of Fyn's flower shop clasping a large bunch of flowers, and run across to the art shop, disappearing inside before Knightly had a chance to wave.

Oliver was wearing a suit, shirt and tie, and a determined expression.

Knightly assumed Oliver had a special party to attend, and walked on, meandering towards the flower shop just in time to see Fyn put the closed sign up.

Popping a piece of treacle toffee in his mouth, Knightly continued along, looking at the shops, and then headed back to the road leading up to the loch.

Chewing his toffee and enjoying the relaxing atmosphere of the loch and surrounding countryside, he noticed Etta coming out of her cottage. She was carrying her craft bag and a large carrot cake on a plate that was covered with a clear cake dome. It looked heavy and awkward to carry, so Knightly hooked his bag of sweets on his arm and ran over to assist her.

'Let me help you with that, Etta.'

'Thanks,' she said, happy to offload the cake to Knightly. 'I would've put the cake in a light paper bag but I've slathered it with buttercream icing and I don't want to mess it up. I baked it for the crafting night at Bee's cottage.'

'Is that where you're heading?' he said.

'Yes, it's on the other side of the loch and up a wee bit into the fields. Not far, if you're sure it's not out of your way.'

'No, I was just out for a walk around the village, and got tempted in by the sweet shop.'

Etta saw the bag he had and laughed.

They walked along the edge of the loch, chatting, and headed up a grassy path that led to Bee's cottage.

'Mullcairn seems interested in you, Etta,' Knightly revealed. 'He wanted to know what you were like in person, as I'd met you.'

Etta was taken aback. 'What did you tell him?'

'I said you were nothing but a troublemaker,' he joked.

Etta laughed. 'Aye, maybe I am. Mullcairn sounds like trouble himself.'

'I think there will be mischief between the two of you when he comes to the fair. And he seems keen to dance with you at the ceilidh.'

'Does he?' She sounded delighted to hear this, but tried to remain unperturbed. 'I'll probably give him a wee dance if he behaves himself.'

Knightly smirked. 'There's little chance of that. Or from you, Etta.'

Laughing and chatting, they headed up the path, into the garden surrounding Bee's cottage. Pretty little solar lights lit the garden of the traditional, white–painted cottage. They walked up to the door. It was open, and chatter sounded from inside.

'I'll carry your cake in for you, and then let you enjoy your night,' said Knightly.

It was a fairly large cottage, and a spare room at the back was set up as Bee's knitting room where she kept her spinning wheel and extensive range of yarn, and the garments she knitted and sold from her website. The ladies were seated there and had brought their knitting, quilting, crochet and other crafts with them.

When Bee and the other ladies saw Knightly, he was welcomed in, and Bee insisted he stay for a cup of tea and a slice of cake. She'd laid on a small selection of sandwiches and other snacks in the kitchen. Aileen was there helping to make the tea, and other ladies were buzzing around setting things up for their crafting and chatter.

Rather than feel like he was in the way, Knightly stayed and fitted right into their lively evening, even giving his opinion on the dresses that Penny had brought with her. A couple of the ladies tried the dresses on in the bedroom and then came through to show the others.

Etta came through wearing a tea dress.

'I was telling Etta that Mullcairn is eager to dance with her at the ceilidh after the fair,' Knightly told them. 'So she needs a dress to impress. And I think that one is lovely. The deep blue colour suits you.'

The other ladies agreed.

Penny checked that it fitted well. 'Yes, it suits you, Etta.'

'I'll take it. What a bargain.'

'I got the dresses for a bargain myself, a whole bundle, so I like to pass the savings on,' said Penny.

Amy arrived, carrying her craft bag and smiled when she saw Knightly. 'Are you here to embroider, or cause mischief?'

'A bit of both.' He held up the plate where he'd been eating a slice of the carrot cake. 'And enjoying a tasty snack. This is delicious, Etta.' Then he offered his bag of sweets around. 'Help yourselves. Sylvia and Muira picked them. There's everything from chocolate truffles to toffee. I can recommend the treacle toffee.'

Sylvia and Muira smiled.

Everyone was having fun, and Bee was learning techniques from Knightly on how to improve her presentations for her knitting videos.

'I feel that my opening introduction doesn't sound as confident as when I start to talk about my knitting or spinning my yarn,' Bee told Knightly.

He remembered that Amy had felt like this, and tried to advise Bee how to improve her introductions. 'I assume you edit your videos.'

'Yes.'

'Start by talking about your knitting,' he advised. 'Then when you've settled into a confident tone, read your introduction. Later, edit it and put the intro at the beginning of your video. Your opening introduction will sound a lot better.'

'I like that idea. Can I try it?' Bee was keen to practise while Knightly was there to give her advice.

'That was better,' he said. 'But try to breathe slower and drop your shoulders down, be less tense.'

Bee tried again and nodded, hearing and feeling the improvement. 'Just a few wee tips from you makes such a difference.'

Knightly showed Bee how to breathe deeper from her core, standing next to her. Bee started giggling, and the ladies were laughing too, when the tall figure of Campbell walked in and glared at Knightly.

Campbell wore a white shirt, dark jeans and sturdy boots.

'This is Campbell.' Bee stepped away from Knightly as she made the introductions, sensing Campbell's feathers were rubbed up the wrong way. 'Knightly is showing us how to improve our video presentations, using his stage acting experience.'

Campbell forced a smile. 'That's helpful of him.'

'More tea?' Aileen suggested and hurried through to the kitchen.

Bee offered up the bag of sweets to Campbell. 'Knightly brought sweeties. Would you like a bon bon?'

Campbell accepted the sweet, popped it in his mouth and chewed on it, and on the thought that Sean had been concerned that Knightly was a bit of a troublemaker. Or at least, a distraction for the ladies. And here Knightly was, part of Bee's crafting evening. Campbell had dropped by to hand in the spindle he'd mended for her. He'd had no intention of staying. Until he'd seen Knightly there.

'You're welcome to join us,' Bee said to Campbell, sure that he'd refuse and be on his way.

Instead, Campbell took her by surprise. 'Yes, I think I will.'

'Etta's home baked carrot cake is delicious,' Knightly recommended.

'I'll have a slice of that with my tea,' said Campbell, and sat down in the hub of them. He'd been working in the fields all day, tending to the beehives, so it seemed fitting he'd end his day at the bee night.

CHAPTER THIRTEEN

Oliver sent a message to Robin:

Don't make dinner. Not sure what I want. I'll be there soon. Love, Oliver x.

Okay. x.

Robin put her phone aside and continued working on the piece of textile art she was making. She'd just mixed the right shade of green for part of a design depicting the castle's forest, and took advantage of finishing it before Oliver arrived.

Oliver scrambled around in his art shop, checking he had everything for the grand proposal. That's how it felt, as if he'd over–egged everything until he was running rings around himself.

He had the ring in his jacket pocket. He checked the ring was inside the velvet box. It was. Phew!

The cake, framed watercolour and flowers were in the boot of the car. He'd checked that twice.

Nodding to himself, he checked his appearance in the mirror and straightened his tie. He had everything, he concluded, except his self composure.

Deep breath. Drive up to Robin's cottage. Dinner. Then propose. That was the plan.

Scurrying out and getting into his car, he drove up to the cottage. The loch was looking particularly scenic. The calm surface was edged with flowers and grass, creating the perfect setting. Stars twinkled in the evening sky.

Hearing Oliver's car pull up outside, Robin stopped working on the textile art and went through to the kitchen to wash her hands.

Oliver left everything in the car and walked in and stood in the doorway of the kitchen, armed with excuses.

Drying her hands, Robin looked round and jolted. 'Wow! Look at you all dressed up in your suit.'

Excuse number one. 'I had to send new publicity pictures to my publisher,' he fibbed. 'I thought I'd go for the dapper look rather than the painterly one for a change.'

'Nice choice. You look like you could walk down a classic fashion runway for menswear.'

Oliver bucked up, pleased that she liked his outfit. 'I decided to keep it on for dinner.'

'Yes,' Robin nodded firmly. 'Why not.' She frowned at her jeans and jumper. 'In comparison, I'm grossly underdressed.'

Under other circumstances he'd have said she looked fine and didn't need to change into anything special. But tonight, he encouraged otherwise. 'Go put something lovely on while I start dinner.'

Robin smiled, keen to do this.

'I'll pop one of those pies with the shortcrust pastry in the oven. Easy–peasy dinner for two,' said Oliver, wangling the pieces of his plan into the winning positions on the chess board.

'Great idea.' Robin beamed a smile at him and then went away through to the bedroom to find something lovely. A couple of dresses sprang to mind.

She'd washed her hair that morning, so all it needed was taken out of the ponytail and brushed.

Watching her leave, Oliver took his jacket off and hung it on the back of a kitchen chair, and set the dinner plan into action. Phase two was going well, he thought, putting the pie in the oven and opening a tin of petit pois and baby carrots to accompany it.

He laid the plates on the kitchen table, adding napkins and making it look inviting. Running out to the garden, he picked a handful of flowers and put them in a glass of water to decorate the table. The bouquet was in the car, but he didn't dare reveal any of his plans.

By the time Robin came back through, the dinner was cooking nicely.

'I was going to wear this to the ceilidh dance after the fair. It's one of Penny's pre–loved vintage dresses.' The mid–calf length midnight blue dress had a layer of dark chiffon scattered with sparkles. Penny had repaired the hem and mended any imperfections on the bodice, adding sequins to create a starry sky effect. 'I think it's beautiful.'

Oliver's heart ached just looking at her. He nodded. 'You're beautiful.'

Robin laughed lightly. 'Will this do for dinner?' She'd worn her hair down and put her makeup on.

'It's perfect for this evening,' he said.

Robin tied a pretty apron on over her dress and helped Oliver serve up the dinner.

They sat down and ate their meal, chatting about their day and her plans for the fair.

As they finished, Robin got up to make the tea.

Oliver stood up. 'Let's take a stroll out by the loch and then come back to have our tea. It's such a lovely evening.'

'Okay,' Robin was happy to agree. 'We're all dressed up so let's go.' She wore the pumps she intended to dance in, and heading out with Oliver.

He'd put his jacket on, and could feel his heart start to thunder in his chest as they walked down to the loch and along to the spot where he'd planned to propose. They had it all to themselves.

They walked along hand in hand, and Robin gazed up at the stars in the sky. 'It's a gorgeous night. I'm glad I decided to spend it with you.'

Oliver stopped and gazed down at her, so tall in stature. Then he got down on one knee, took the velvet box from his jacket pocket and opened it to reveal the ring.Robin gasped, completely taken aback, seeing the scintillating solitaire diamond looking even more like white fire in the glow of the evening light.

Hoping he didn't falter over his words, Oliver proposed. 'Will you marry me, Robin?' He'd decided not to say anything other than what he wanted more than anything.

His heart seemed to stop, his whole world paused, waiting on Robin's reply.He'd taken her aback so strongly, that her own heart was beating fast, but full of love for this wonderful man.

'Yes,' she said, breathlessly, letting her acceptance burst from her lips before she smiled at him.

Feeling the relief of the thousands of hours of pent up tension release with her one heartfelt word, he took the ring from the box and placed it on her engagement finger.

The white gold setting enhanced the sparkle as she looked at it on her ring finger, still hardly believing this was true.

Standing up, Oliver pulled her close and kissed her.

'I love you so much,' he said.

'I love you too, Oliver. I never expected this.' The tensions in him recently made sense now, though he'd planned and hid his plan well.

'I think we should try that dress of yours for a first dance,' he told her.

Letting him take her in hold, they waltzed to the silent tune of their hearts beating as one by the side of the beautiful Scottish loch.

Then Oliver led her back up to the cottage. 'I've a few other small surprises for you.' Opening the boot of the car, he lifted out the watercolour and handed it to her.

'You painted the engagement ring!' She sounded so delighted. 'I love this. It's going up on the cottage wall tonight!'

One successful gift down, he then presented her with the bouquet of flowers.

'Oh, these smell gorgeous,' she said.

The final surprise was the heart–shaped engagement cake.

Robin read the words: Will you marry me, Robin?

'I asked Bradoch to make it,' he said. She'd already accepted his proposal, but it was nice to have it written in icing on top of the cake.

'We need photos of this, all of these, and us. You can set the timer on the camera to capture us both.' The excitement in Robin's voice sounded in the calm night air.

Hurrying inside the cottage, eager to take a look at the cake and the painting in the lights of the living room, Robin's enthusiasm was clear for Oliver to see. To his relief, Robin had accepted his proposal, with bells on.

Oliver carried the cake inside the cottage.

Closing the cottage door to their past, as Robin rushed ahead with the painting and the bouquet, admiring her ring, he felt their future just beginning.

Robin hoped she hadn't gone overboard with the photos, but surely they couldn't have enough pictures of their engagement night.

She'd wanted pictures taken outside by the loch where Oliver had proposed. He'd been happy to go along with everything.

'I know there will be enough to make an album, but I don't care,' Robin said, giggling. 'Stand in front of the loch, so I can take a snap of you in your smart suit.'

Oliver happily posed for her.

She eyed him with suspicion. 'Were you really having press pictures taken?'

He smiled and shook his head, causing her to smile even more.

'And the pies in the freezer and groceries?'

He shrugged and grinned.

'Rascal. I bet you were doing more than just painting the other day,' she surmised.

'Oh, yes,' he agreed. He wanted to tell her more about the cake planning, but was worried he'd let slip about Neil's proposal that was due the following night. So he kept this to himself. He'd tell her the whole story when Neil and Penny were engaged.

An unintentional spindle contest was underway between Knightly and Campbell.

Knightly had been encouraged to have a go at spinning his own yarn using one of Bee's small, hand held, drop spindles. Always keen to have a go at things, Knightly had thrown himself into the task, laughing as he got his strands of yarn in a mess.

'I've got myself in a fankle.' Knightly held the spindle up with the woolly tangle dangling from it. 'But I'll have another go if someone would be so kind as to unravel me.'

The ladies were laughing, and Bee helped Knightly start again.

'Round two,' Knightly announced.

Campbell was having better luck with his, taking his time and managing to tease the wool fibres gently as he spun the spindle. The strand of new fibres wound around the spindle, creating a length of hand spun yarn.

Knightly faired well on his second attempt, matching Campbell's effort.

Now the competition started to hot up.

The ladies could see Campbell's frustration at Knightly's new–found ability.

'I'm getting the hang of this now,' said Knightly, sounding chirpy. 'Oh, look, I've spun a whole length of my own yarn without knotting it. This is fun.'

'It takes practise,' said Bee, hoping her calm tone would allay the competitiveness. 'But once you learn the technique, it's quite relaxing, and lovely to create your own yarn using a wee drop spindle.'

Campbell was adept at handling the beehives, but he was used to wearing the gauntlets. He concentrated and made an impressive effort, winding enough yarn around the spindle to show that he'd learned how to do it. Finishing, he handed the spindle to Bee. 'Marks out of ten.'

'Top marks,' Bee announced with a smile, causing Campbell's serious expression to ease into a relieved grin.

'Oops! Fiddled the fibres there, but...yes, it's still one strand,' said Knightly.

'Top marks all round,' said Bee, preventing further competition.

'Are you demonstrating spinning your own yarn at the fair?' Knightly said to Bee.

'Yes, I'm taking my spinning wheel with me,' said Bee. 'But I'll take several of the small hand held drop spindles to let people have a go at hand spinning.'

The ladies began to discuss what they were demonstrating while Bee put the kettle on to make another round of tea. Muira went through to the kitchen to give her a hand.

'I was thinking of preparing my embroidery patterns, drawing the three designs on to the fabric and putting them in the hoops ready for the fair,' Knightly said to Amy. 'But I'm one hoop short. Any chance I could borrow a third hoop? I have one for my signature. And a slightly bigger one for the crewel bumblebee.'

Knightly didn't have his embroidery with him, but Amy rummaged through her bag and found a spare hoop. 'Your acorn pattern will fit into this one.' She handed it to him.

'Great.' Knightly reached over and grabbed the empty sweet shop bag from the table, shook any remnants of chocolate from it, and put the hoop inside ready to take with him. 'And do you have any spare pieces of white fabric? I think I've got enough at the cabin, but just in case I mess up drawing the designs on to the fabric,' said Knightly.

Amy was happy to give him extra pieces of fabric that she had in her bag. And she was impressed that he had a plan to prepare the patterns in the hoops.

'I won't finish embroidering any of the three patterns at the Saturday afternoon demonstration,' Knightly told Amy. 'But it'll let me continue them on the Sunday. And if one goes horribly wrong, I can hide it and make a show of the remaining two.'

Amy beamed a warm smile at Knightly that he reflected back at her.

Campbell could see the connection between Knightly and Amy. Though neither of them seemed to be taking things further. Sighing at his own silly behaviour, he got up and went through to the kitchen. Putting his arms around Bee as she stood at the kitchen table setting the cups up, he whispered to her. 'Sorry for...' *Being jealous, challenging Knightly, acting like a fool.* 'Everything tonight.'

Bee leaned back, snuggling into him, feeling his strong arms around her.

This was all the reassurance Campbell needed that he'd been forgiven for his foolishness.

Campbell helped Muira and Bee carry the tea through to the ladies. The remainder of their evening was filled with chatting about their craft demonstrations for the fair.

'You should certainly demonstrate knitting one of your lace shawls,' Etta said to Bee.

Bee agreed. She could knit this at speed and with accuracy, so it would be quite interesting to show her knitting skills. Her lace knitting videos on her website were always popular.

'Are you going to demonstrate knitting cables on jumpers?' Bee remembered Etta mentioning about this.

'I am,' Etta confirmed. 'Probably on an Aran knit jumper.'

'I'm going to demonstrate knitting a Fair Isle jumper,' Bee added.

Jessy spoke up. 'Elspeth and Kity have confirmed they're taking part in the demonstrations. Elspeth said that she was thinking of knitting a robin softie and an owl.'

'Elspeth's knitted softies are lovely,' said Bee. 'She puts them in the window of her knitting shop on the island to promote the yarn for sale, but customers buy them.'

'I'd love to knit a robin,' said Sylvia. 'I must see how Elspeth knits one at the fair.'

'Check Elspeth's website,' Bee advised Sylvia. 'She has patterns for the softies she designs on her website.'

'I'll have a peek.' Sylvia looked up the website on her phone.

'I promised Elspeth I'd give her a call tonight so she could discuss her plans with us.' Etta phoned her.

'Hello, Etta,' Elspeth said, smiling out the phone. 'Are you at Bee's cottage?'

'I am,' Etta confirmed and held the phone to show Elspeth the ladies smiling and waving to her. Knightly joined in.

'I see you have company,' Elspeth remarked, noticing Knightly.

'Yes, Knightly and Campbell are here.' Etta gave a brief explanation of what they were up to.

'It sounds like a fun night,' said Elspeth.

'Jessy was just saying you're thinking of demonstrating knitting a robin softie and an owl,' Etta prompted Elspeth.

'Yes,' Elspeth confirmed. 'I'll have other knitting on the go at my stall, like a hat and scarf, but my customers love the softies. The owl is knitted in autumn tones, amber, yellow ochre and chocolate. I thought this would suit this time of year.'

'That'll be ideal,' said Etta.

'Your delivery arrived at my cottage,' Bee told Elspeth. 'I've stored it in the spare bedroom.' Bee had this room ready for Elspeth.

'Thanks,' said Elspeth. 'I've got my car packed with yarn. I'm driving over on the ferry first thing in the morning. I'm planning an early night.'

'We'll not keep you,' said Etta. 'Get a good night's sleep and we'll see you when you arrive tomorrow. Kity is arriving then too at my cottage.'

Elspeth smiled and waved at them as the call ended.

The chatter continued about their plans. The ladies discussed demonstrating a wide range of crafts, including crochet, needle felting, cross stitching, tapestry, rag doll making and dressmaking.

'What type of embroidery are you demonstrating?' Muira said to Amy.

'A bee garden scene with sunflowers, daisies, foxgloves, cornflowers, wee beehives and bees buzzing around the flowers. It'll let me show various stitches using stranded cotton thread,' said Amy. 'A large crewelwork thistle. The crewel wool creates a lovely fluffy top to the thistle. And I was thinking of including a goldwork embroidery, a leaf demonstration using closed fly stitch, especially now that Knightly is showing three different knitting patterns.' She smiled over at Knightly.

'Better up your game, Amy,' Knightly said, jokingly. 'And what is goldwork embroidery?'

'Embroidery using metallic threads,' Amy explained to Knightly.

They continued to talk about their demonstrations, and Knightly advised them on how to present themselves well at their stalls.

The evening finally came to a close, with everyone heading home, offering lifts to each other or walking back along the loch.

'Would you like a lift back to the castle with Jessy and me?' Amy said to Knightly.

'Yes, thank you.' He took his hoop in the paper bag and pieces of fabric with him.

'We'll need to get you a proper craft bag,' Amy said to Knightly.

Jessy agreed. 'You can't turn up at the fair carrying a paper poke.'

'I'll sort one out for you,' Amy told him.

'I don't want to cause any more fuss,' he said.

'No fuss at all,' Amy assured him. 'I have a spare craft tote you can use. I'll drop it off at your cabin.'

Knightly sat in the back seat, and the three of them chatted on the short drive up to the castle's estate.

'I'm planning to get an early night tomorrow evening,' said Jessy. 'I'll be up early to work at the castle and help with the fair.'

'Not long now,' said Knightly.

'Feeling nervous?' Amy said to him as she drove towards his cabin.

'No, luckily, I've never been one to have stage jitters,' he said. The main thing that unnerved him was the thought that Amy would be leaving to go back home soon.

'Do you think you'll extend your stay here after the fair?' Knightly said to Amy, with hope in his voice.

'No, I'll attend the ceilidh dance on the Sunday night,' she said. 'Then I'll pack up and drive home on the Monday morning.'

Knightly kept the smile on his face, acting well, even though the thought of her leaving cut his heart to the core. 'Well, I'm sure you'll take lots of happy memories with you.'

'I will,' Amy told him. But it was what she was leaving behind that made her heart ache — Knightly, and the chance of romance.

CHAPTER FOURTEEN

Oliver put the watercolour painting of Robin's engagement ring in the window of his art shop.

Robin was happy for him to display it for a week, as a way to announce their engagement to the village, and then it would be hung up in the living room of her cottage.

Oliver popped across to the bakery.

Bradoch saw the smile on Oliver's face. 'I see that congratulations are in order.'

'Robin loved the cake.'

'Would it be okay if I put a picture of the cake on the bakery website?' said Bradoch.

'Yes, and I'll give you a picture of us with the cake if you want,' Oliver offered.

Bradoch nodded firmly. 'That would be great.'

Oliver scrolled through the pictures on his phone, selected two that Bradoch could have, and sent them to him.

'I'll use both of them,' said Bradoch.

Heading back over to the art shop with two fresh baked morning rolls for his breakfast, Oliver felt that the world was a shinier place. Robin had accepted his proposal. It was going to take a wee while, he thought, for the elation to wane.

Putting the kettle on for tea, Oliver buttered the rolls and then phoned Neil.

'Robin thinks the ring is beautiful,' said Oliver. 'It was sparkling like white fire last night by the loch. And it's a perfect fit.'

'I'm delighted she loves the ring. And I'm happy for the two of you,' said Neil.

Aileen phoned Etta. 'I've got some lovely fabric that would be nice for a wedding quilt.'

It was customary for a wedding quilt to be given to any local couple of their acquaintance on their engagement.

Aileen had a couple of bolts of cotton quilting weight fabric on the counter. 'One has a wee robin design. It's just in for my Christmas range, but I thought it would be a nod to Robin's name. And it's a pretty fabric. Come down and have a look when you've got time.'

'I'll pop down the now,' said Etta. 'It's so exciting. They'll make a lovely couple.'

'They will,' Aileen agreed. 'I'm hoping Robin will tell us all the details of Oliver's proposal.'

'I phoned to congratulate her, and she says her phone is buzzing. So I was thinking we'll have a wee celebration after the fair,' Etta suggested.

'Oliver cut it close to the fair. At least he proposed last night rather than this evening,' said Aileen.

'Yes, we're all so busy. Kity arrives here this afternoon.'

'I'll put the kettle on. Come and have a quick cuppa with me and help me select the fabric for the wedding quilt.'

Etta walked down from her cottage to the main street. She saw the ring painting in Oliver's art shop and stopped to admire it. Robin had told her about it. Then she hurried on to Aileen's quilt shop.

'I see Oliver's got the watercolour of the engagement ring in his shop window,' Etta commented as she went inside.

Aileen perked up. 'Has he? I'll be back in a jiffy. I want to have a look.' And off she ran to peek in the art shop window.

Hearing the kettle click off, Etta made the tea in time for Aileen to come dashing back in.

'It's a sparkler of a solitaire diamond with a band of white gold.' Aileen was clearly impressed. 'I love solitaire engagement rings.'

'Traditional and classy,' said Etta, handing a cup of tea to Aileen.

'Thanks for making the tea,' Aileen said, laughing. 'You can tell I'm in a tizzy.'

'We're all taken aback by the surprise engagement. Imagine how Robin must feel.'

Aileen nodded. 'Especially as the craft fair is tomorrow. What a whirlwind of excitement.'

Messages from well–wishers were starting to pop up on Oliver's phone, and Robin called to say that Etta had heard the news and it was now circulating through the members of the crafting bee.

Oliver phoned Walter to tell him that the engagement was no longer a secret and he could tell Gaven and others.

And then Oliver sat down in the little kitchen at the back of the art shop, sipping his tea and eating his rolls, unable to stop smiling to himself every time he thought about Robin agreeing to be his wife.

Amy was in an embroidery bubble of her own, unaware of the news. Jessy had already left to walk to work at the castle before Amy was awake.

Hearing the news from Walter, Jessy decided to tell Amy later, letting her have a long lie in. It was going to be a hectic time at the fair the following day.

Amy had woken up not long after Jessy left, jumped in the shower, got dressed, made tea and porridge for breakfast, and then started work on the embroidery patterns she'd decided to demonstrate at the fair.

She'd sewn them all before, and they were her own designs, but she had fresh ideas for the colours of the threads for the bee garden pattern. And, like Knightly, she drew the patterns on to the fabric and put them in the hoops ready for embroidering.

A vintage denim tote bag sat in the living room ready to hand in to Knightly's cabin. She planned to do that later, nearer lunchtime, and concentrated on getting her embroidery ready for the demonstrations.

Knightly gave himself three gold stars. He wouldn't boast to Amy or anyone else, but he'd drawn the three patterns on to fabric and they were now securely in three hoops ready for embroidering. He hadn't messed up any of them. Phew! It had been tense when he almost messed up his bumble.

The signature was easy. He'd just signed his name clearly. The acorns were fairly easy too, but the bumblebee was tricky.

But they were done, and he put them in the empty sweetie bag for safe keeping, wondering if Amy would remember she'd promised him a craft bag.

'The robin fabric is gorgeous,' Etta agreed. 'And I like this print with tiny artist palettes and brushes, like a nod to Oliver's art. The colours are nice and bright and suit the pattern of the robins.'

'The white and pale pastel background make the colours of the designs pop,' said Aileen.

'I like this vintage tea shop print with teapots, cups, cakes and bunting.' Etta admired the fabric.

'These three would make a wonderful quilt with some colour matched solids,' said Aileen. 'We could use the robin print for the backing fabric.'

'Yes, I like that mix,' said Etta.

Aileen took a picture of the three fabrics. 'I'll message a few of the other ladies, and if we're all agreed, this is what we'll use to make Robin and Oliver's wedding quilt.'

Neil walked along to Penny's cottage after breakfast, hoping to talk to her about their plans for dinner.

The front door was open and he could hear the busy chatter coming from inside as a few ladies, including Bee and Muira, collected the dresses they'd bought for the ceilidh.

Penny was packing the items she intended taking to the castle to set up her stall, putting them into the back of her car.

The chatter circulated around the new engagement and the dresses. Neil felt like he was an intrusion before Penny had even seen him approaching. He stopped, overhearing their conversation, wondering if he should message Penny instead of interrupting her busy day.

'Robin had no idea that Oliver was planning to propose to her,' Penny said to Bee.

'What a surprise she must've got,' said Bee.

'I was talking to Aileen,' Muira told them. 'She says Oliver cut it close to the fair. But at least he proposed last night and not this evening.'

'Yes,' Penny agreed.

Alarm bells rang loud and clear through Neil. He turned around and headed back to his cottage without Penny or the others seeing him. Doubt pressed down around his shoulders, feeling like a heavy weight of tension.

Closing his cottage door, he went through to his kitchen and sat down, rethinking his plans. Making a cup of tea settled his nerves. Don't get the jitters now, he warned himself. Stick to the plan.

'Oliver has put a painting of the engagement ring in the window of his art shop,' Muira said to Penny, continuing their conversation. 'I ran over from the sweetie shop for a peek. It's a stoater of a diamond.'

'I can't wait to see the ring,' said Penny.

'Robin's heading up to the castle,' Bee told her. 'We'll see it there. I'm driving up as soon as I drop my dress off at the cottage. Thanks again for adding the sequins around the neckline. It makes it look like I'm wearing a sparkly necklace.'

'I'm pleased you like it,' said Penny.

Muira looked thoughtful. 'Did Neil design the engagement ring?'

Penny blinked. 'I don't know. He never said anything to me.'

'We'll talk to Robin up at the castle,' Bee concluded.

Sylvia and I are working in our shop today, but we're going up to the marquee when we close tonight,' Muira told them. 'Aileen says she's doing the same after she closes the quilt shop.'

'Did you get Aileen's message about the wedding quilt fabric?' Penny said to them.

'Yes, I love her selection,' said Bee.

Muira agreed. 'The robin fabric is a nice touch.'

The stalls were all set up in the marquees. Bunting had been draped outside the entrance and fluttered in the light breeze. The day promised to be another mild, sunny one, and the forecast for the whole weekend was the same.

The marquees looked wonderful against the backdrop of the castle and the estate, with a bright blue sky above them.

Staff from the castle were milling around along with the stallholders and others participating in the fair.

Penny drove up and started to take dresses, jackets and other garments inside to her stall. Neil had promised to be there on the day to help her, but she planned to get her stall ready today. Jessy had told the bee members that they were welcome to set up today rather than early the following morning. This suited a lot of the ladies.

Bee arrived with Campbell. He carried her spinning wheel inside the marquee and put it at her stall. They'd brought the delivery of Elspeth's yarn and put it on her stall ready for her arrival in the afternoon.

Walter helped the ladies with everything from carrying stuff for them to putting up their banners.

The marquees were abuzz with activity, and news of the engagement circulated around the stallholders, with Robin being congratulated by numerous members of the community, including Bee and Penny.

'It's a gorgeous ring,' Bee said to Robin.

Penny agreed.

'Oliver bought it from Neil,' Robin revealed.

'Neil designed your engagement ring?' said Penny. 'I didn't know that.'

'Apparently Oliver and Neil had kept it a secret,' said Robin. 'But Bradoch knew because he'd obviously made the cake. There are pictures of the cake up on the bakery's website if you want a peek.'

They did, and gazed with interest as Robin showed them on her phone. 'Bradoch even iced the message on the cake.'

'What a lovely idea,' said Penny.

'I like the heart–shape design,' Bee remarked. 'So romantic.'

They continued to set up their stalls, but Penny sent a message to Neil:

You designed Robin's engagement ring!
I promised Oliver I'd keep it a secret.

Penny understood. *Everyone loves the ring. It's a beautiful design. I'm setting up my stall at the castle.*

Do you need me to help you set it up?

No, it's fine. You get on with your work. Come and help me during the fair.

I'm looking forward to seeing you tonight for dinner.

We'll have a relaxing evening.

Neil smiled to himself. *See you tonight.*

Knightly walked into the castle to have a late breakfast. Gaven, Walter and another man, the same age and height as the laird, were deep in conversation, but Gaven smiled when he saw Knightly.

'Ah, Knightly, come and meet Struan.' Gaven beckoned him over to join them and the introductions were made.

Knightly remembered the name and smiled. 'I believe you're responsible for my demonstrations being highlighted on the castle's website.' His tone was light–hearted.

'Yes,' said Struan, grinning. 'All a bit of crossed wires.' He glanced at Gaven. 'Entirely my fault.' Gaven smiled, taking the blame. 'But now Knightly's our star attraction at the fair.'

Knightly laughed.

Amid the jovial chat, fuller introductions were made.

'Struan owns the Christmas Cake Chateau hotel further north in the Highlands,' said Gaven. 'It's known as this because it looks like a white iced Christmas cake.'

Struan had stunning blue eyes, well–styled dark hair, and his suit looked like money and class.

Knightly and Struan shook hands and smiled.

Gaven continued the introductions. 'Struan's visiting us for the fair.' He explained they'd been friends for years and helped each other promote their hotel facilities. 'The chateau was used as a location recently for a Hollywood film.'

Knightly's recall sparked. 'Oh, yes, I heard about that in the press. I saw that film. Didn't you get roped in to perform some of the action scenes when the leading man, Sanderson Sanders, did himself a mischief during rehearsals?'

Struan smiled. 'I did.'

'Struan's become infamous for that scene where he slid down the balustrade of the chateau's staircase in tight swashbuckling trousers,' said Gaven.

'The wardrobe assistants had to stitch Struan into the trousers,' Walter chipped–in.

'And afterwards, they had to cut him free from them,' Gaven elaborated, causing them all to laugh.

'Happy memories I'd rather forget,' said Struan.

'And Struan was the man who jumped off the roof of the chateau at the exciting end of the film,' Gaven reminded him.

Knightly's eyes widened. 'Was that you?'

Struan nodded, reluctant to take much credit. 'I'm just happy now running my chateau and passing the baton to Gaven. A film company are interested in using the castle as a location.'

'I've put them off until the New Year,' Gaven told Knightly. 'I don't want the filming to interrupt our parties for the festive season and the Christmas ball at the castle.'

'But you'll be letting them film at the castle next year?' Knightly wanted to clarify.

'Yes, probably. I've invited them to come here for a chat after Christmastime,' said Gaven. 'Come and stay while they're here and I'll introduce you. Maybe you'll be the next volunteer to swash his buckle on the silver screen.'

Knightly laughed. 'I've always stuck to my theatre work.'

'Well, come along anyway,' said Gaven.

'It's an exciting action drama involving ballroom dancing,' Struan told Knightly. 'Are you a ballroom dancer?'

'I can do ballroom. I went to stage school,' Knightly explained. 'I learned to act, dance, sing...and now I've learned how to embroider.'

'And he's performing a Highland Fling at the fair,' Walter added.

They all laughed.

'Shall we go through to the dining room for breakfast?' said Gaven, beckoning to Struan and Knightly.

Leaving Walter to tend to guests at reception, they went through and were seated at Gaven's table where they were served full breakfasts that included scrambled eggs, grilled tomatoes, toast and tea, and continued their conversation.

'Knightly is staying in one of the luxury cabins on a creative break,' Gaven told Struan.

'And thoroughly enjoying it,' said Knightly, cutting into his toast and scooping up some scrambled eggs.

Struan cupped his tea. 'I'm thinking of extending the chateau's facilities to include cabins for guests,' said Struan.

Gaven finished a mouthful of toast. 'We're adding several new cabins to the estate,' he said to Knightly. 'Campbell is helping with the architectural designs.'

'The estate is a beautiful location,' said Knightly. 'I've wandered through parts of it, and there's so much more to see. And the loch is lovely.'

'Are you tempted to stay here in the village?' said Struan, tucking into his eggs and toast.

'Tempted,' Knightly admitted, then shook his head. 'But my theatre roles demand I work in Edinburgh.'

'Pop back when you can for visits,' Gaven encouraged Knightly.

'And if you're up north, come and stay at the chateau,' Struan added.

'I'll do that,' Knightly promised both of them.

Amy picked up two bags filled with her embroidery, and the vintage denim tote bag, and walked from Jessy's cottage along to Knightly's cabin.

She knocked on the door, but he wasn't in.

Walking away, she headed to the marquee to find her stall and start arranging her embroidery work on display.

The marquees looked wonderful as she walked towards them, feeling a wave of excitement, seeing people taking boxes and bags from their cars and carrying them into the huge tents.

Amy walked inside the main marquee and gazed up at the lights draped across the interior, creating a bright and airy atmosphere. The friendly buzz of voices, eagerly setting up their displays, enhanced the sense of excitement building.

Jessy saw Amy and waved to her. 'Your stall is over here.'

Amy threaded her way across the centre of the marquee to where Jessy and others, including Etta, Bee, Robin and Penny were busy unpacking items for sale.

Amy's stall was tucked into this niche and was fairly close to the small stage that Walter had built for Knightly's performances. She glanced around, but there was no sign of Knightly, and she assumed he was either in the castle or out walking, exploring the estate.

Shrugging the bags off her shoulders, Amy started to unpack her embroidery, while joining in the chatter, and soon found out the news about Robin's engagement.

'Congratulations,' Amy said to Robin, admiring the ring, and receiving a wish on it.

Turning the ring three times around her own ring finger, Amy made her wish and then handed the solitaire sparkler back to Robin.

'I hope your wish comes true,' Robin said, smiling at Amy.

Amy smiled, but doubted it would. Her life didn't have room for romance right now, and it would soon be time for her to go back home. She wasn't melancholy about going home. She loved her small but cosy home and knew she'd be happy to be back once she was there.

It was the prospect of ending her time with Knightly that stressed her. The closer it came to leaving, the more she realised this was what was troubling her. Jessy would visit her in the town, and they'd keep in touch, but Jessy had her own life in the village. A happy life. A busy life too. Jessy was busy with her work at the castle most days, and attended the crafting bee nights. Amy's life in the town was emptier. But she was a homebody at heart.

Amy hung the denim bag at the side of her stall, and concentrated on presenting her embroidery to show her designs. Most of them were displayed in hoops and could be hung up, like embroidered pictures, on a wall. She sold kits containing everything needed to create an embroidered design, from the pattern to the fabric and thread. Hoops were optional.

Penny came over to look at the range of embroidery thread that Amy curated. Some were a mix of stranded cotton embroidery thread that she'd handpicked in a specific colour range. Others were threads Amy had hand–dyed herself. This was something she did at home, and another reason for going back to the town where she could restock her own colours.

'I don't want to spoil your display,' Penny began. 'But I've bought your handpicked collections of thread before and I'd like to buy more while you're here. And the hand–dyed threads.'

'Select what you want, Penny,' Amy encouraged her. 'I brought plenty of thread with me in my car. This is just what I brought with me this morning.'

Penny perked up, and started to buy a selection of the embroidery thread. 'I use a lot of these for my sewing and mending.'

Robin joined in, wanting several skeins of Amy's new autumn colours.

While Amy was dealing with Penny and Robin, she saw Knightly walk into the marquee, accompanied by Gaven, Walter and another man.

'That's Struan,' Jessy whispered to Amy, and explained why Struan was there.

Knightly glanced around, but there were so many busy stalls that he didn't see Amy. She wondered if she'd imagined the disappointment on his face.

Tempted to wave over to him, she decided to forgo interrupting him, because clearly Walter wanted to show him the stage, and Gaven and Struan were interested in this too.

She'd see Knightly later, Amy consoled herself.

Jessy went over to check that everything was in order with the stage, leaving Amy and the others to continue working at their stalls.

Amy kept glancing over, seeing Knightly now talking to Jessy. Her aunt pointed over to Amy's stall, but other things were in the way, including more bunting being hung, so he didn't see her exact location.

A short time later, Jessy came back and smiled at Amy and the other ladies.

'Chef needs volunteers to taste test his new blend of hot chocolate,' Jessy told them. Chef will be organising various stalls for snacks and refreshments for the fair. But this is his chocolate stall. He wants to test his mix. So I thought we'd volunteer.'

Etta put the knitted jumpers down on the table where she was trying to show them to full advantage at her stall. 'I suppose I could force myself to have a hot chocolate.'

The others nodded, and then they burst out laughing and headed out of the marquee to help chef.

The giggling alerted Knightly's attention, and he caught a glimpse of Amy leaving with the other ladies. He pondered whether to run after her, but clearly they were all happily busy, so he stayed where he was with Gaven, Struan and Walter.

'Music will play on cue,' Walter told Knightly. 'Give a nod when you're ready to do your fling, and it'll be played over the sound system.'

Knightly acknowledged this, but his mind kept thinking about Amy. The time was sparking in too quick. Now he was discussing his dance music. He wanted to rewind the time he'd had with Amy, maybe making more of their quiet moments together where he could've revealed how much he liked her.

Mentally kicking himself for the missed chances, Knightly focussed on what Walter was saying.

'That's great, Walter. You've made a fine job of the stage,' Knightly told him.

Walter's chest puffed up. 'I tried my best to make it sturdy for you.'

During breakfast, Struan had been discussing the style of Knightly's cabin. The designs varied, and he was trying to decide what style would be suitable for the chateau.

'When we're finished here,' said Struan. 'Can I have a look inside your cabin?'

'Yes,' said Knightly. 'We're more or less finished here now. Walter's sorted out the stage. I don't need any adjustments to it. Want to pop along?'

Accepting Knightly's offer, Struan went along to the cabin, while Walter and Gaven became wrapped up in the organising of the marquees.

'Are you looking for someone?' Struan said to Knightly as they walked out of the marquee and towards the cabin. He'd noticed Knightly glancing around, trying to see where Amy was.

There was no sign of her. 'No, just admiring everything,' Knightly lied, and then continued on to the cabin to show Struan around.

'Lucy would love this,' Struan said, admiring the cabin. He was referring to his fiancée. 'I'd hoped she could come with me to the fair, but she's on a book deadline this weekend.'

'Is she an author?' said Knightly.

'No, she's a colouring book artist. That's how we first met. Lucy came to stay in one of the cottages on the chateau's grounds that are extra accommodation for guests. She'd booked a relaxing stay to finish the illustrations for one of her colouring books. But Lucy didn't get a chance to relax. Long story, happy ending.'

'I'm glad it worked out for the two of you.'

Struan smiled. 'I'll let you get on with your day. Thanks for letting me see your cabin. I have a few cottages for guests at the chateau, but I'd like to extend those facilities. That's why I'm interested in the cabins.'

'I'm enjoying my stay here,' Knightly confirmed.

Struan stepped outside. 'I'll find my own way back. Thanks again.'

And Struan left, heading back to the castle.

By the late afternoon, Elspeth and Kity had arrived in the village.

Elspeth was unpacking her bags at Bee's cottage.

Kity sat having a cup of tea in Etta's kitchen.

'I thought with you travelling, driving all the way here from the west coast, and not having a proper lunch, I'd make us an earlier dinner,' said Etta, preparing a tasty dinner for the two of them. She peeled the potatoes for mashing.

Kity relaxed back in her chair, drinking her tea. 'Thanks Etta, and I appreciate you letting me stay with you.'

Sean phoned Muira at the sweet shop in the late afternoon.

Muira and Sylvia were aiming to head to the castle and set up their stall when they'd closed the shop for the day.

'Any plans for your dinner tonight?' Sean said to Muira.

'A run round the kitchen table after we shut the shop,' Muira said lightly.

'Come and run round my kitchen table,' said Sean. 'I'm making a roast with all the trimmings. Plenty to share. Bring Sylvia with you.'

'Oh, that would be so handy. We've had such a busy day in the shop, and now we've a busy night at the castle too.'

'Come round when you've locked up. Then I'll drive up to the castle with you and help out.'

'Thanks, Sean. We'll see you later.'

Campbell came wandering into the kitchen as Sean finished the call.

'Elspeth is settling into Bee's cottage. I'm letting them sort things out without me hanging around,' said Campbell, sitting down at the kitchen table.

'Does Bee have plans for their dinner?'

'Not that I know of, why?'

'Phone Bee and invite her to bring Elspeth over to us for their dinner.' Sean explained he'd invited Muira and Sylvia.

'Great!' Campbell phoned Bee while Sean started to prepare the roasting tin and select the vegetables — potatoes, carrots, parsnips and onions.

'Yes, Elspeth and I would be delighted to join you for dinner,' Bee said to Campbell.

After the call, Campbell smiled at Sean. 'You've got a full house for dinner tonight.'

Sean grinned. 'Wash your hands, roll your sleeves up, and help me prepare the vegetables while I start cooking the roast.'

Campbell was happy to help his father, and they spoke about their bees, the craft fair, and Robin and

Oliver's surprise engagement, while they worked in tandem getting the dinner ready for the ladies.

CHAPTER FIFTEEN

Neil's cottage shone a warm welcome in the golden hour glow of the autumn evening. The front door was open and the light from inside poured out into the garden. The loch looked calm, like Neil, but under the surface of his white shirt, blue silk tie that matched his eyes, grey waistcoat and black trousers, were ripples of excitement and trepidation.

All day, he'd prepared for the proposal night. Dinner was cooking nicely in the oven. The kitchen table was set with a white linen table cover and napkins. A candle flickered in a glass holder, silver cutlery reflected the candlelight, a bottle of champagne was chilling in the fridge and glass flutes were ready to be filled in celebration. If Penny accepted his proposal.

Pushing his doubts aside, so that he wasn't wearing a frown when she arrived, he glanced outside the kitchen window. He wouldn't turn the twinkle lights on yet, but he'd opened the back door and the scent of the flowers from the garden drifted in and mingled with the delicious aroma of the dinner cooking.

As planned, he'd prepared a savoury pie with puff pastry and roast potatoes, with various trimmings, including Penny's favourite cranberry sauce. It felt like Christmas in autumn. And just as exciting as opening gifts on Christmas morning. The ring box was ready to be opened to present Penny with the diamond cluster engagement ring. Polished to perfection. Every bit of his goldsmith skill had gone into it.

He'd hidden the engagement cake, on its silver cake stand, in the pantry cupboard, along with the ribbon–tied cake slice. If Penny said yes.

Stop it! Neil scolded himself. There was no room for doubts. He had to believe that Penny loved him enough to accept his proposal. Any minute now, she'd be here. Any minute now...

'Dinner smells delicious.' Penny's voice rang through to the kitchen as she walked into the hall. She'd been up at the castle for most of the day, then came down to get changed for dinner. Neil had sounded as if he was making an effort to cook a lovely dinner for them, so she'd made an effort too.

Wearing a ditsy floral wrap dress, a vintage find she'd rescued and repaired, that was comfy but pretty, she walked in, smiling. Her blonde hair hung smooth around her shoulders, and she'd emphasised her grey eyes with a brush of mascara.

Neil didn't do casual when it came to his clothes. So Penny didn't think anything special was happening because of his classy attire. But the kitchen table told a different story.

'Oh! This looks romantic,' she said.

Neil's heart lifted a notch. 'Take a seat and I'll serve dinner.'

Penny sat down. 'I've been running around all day, but the stall looks great in the marquee. I'm near Etta, Aileen, Bee and Robin, and other members of the crafting bee, so we'll be able to help each other during the fair. And you'll be there too.'

'I will.' Wearing oven mitts, he pulled the pie out of the oven. The puff pastry was cooked to a light golden perfection. He started to serve it up, along with a selection of vegetables and roast potatoes.

Penny continued to chatter about her day, and kept circulating around to the topic of Robin and Oliver's engagement.

Neil kept turning the topic back to her sewing and mending, not wanting any talk of their surprise engagement to overlap into his surprise proposal.

Penny didn't notice him keeping the conversation focussed on her work, her crafting, and was happy to chat about the vintage dresses the ladies had bought for the ceilidh.

'I inadvertently sold a dress I intended to wear to the ceilidh,' she said, smiling. 'But it suits Aileen, and I didn't like to take it back off her when she wanted it.'

Neil smiled and served up their dinner.

Penny picked up a napkin. 'This looks so tasty.'

He gestured to the cranberry sauce.

'You've thought of everything.' She scooped up a portion of the sauce on to her plate and started to eat her dinner. 'I've been so busy, I've hardly eaten anything all day. Though I did have chef's hot chocolate.'

Neil watched her enjoy her meal as she chatted happily, completely unaware of his plan.

'What were you working on today?' she said, realising she'd barely stopped talking about her day.

'Something special,' he said. 'A ring. Making sure the lustre of the diamonds and gold was perfect.'

'It sounds beautiful,' she said. No hint that she imagined the ring was for her.

'I think it's the most beautiful ring I've ever made.'

'Can I have a peek? Or did the courier come to pick it up for your customer?'

'I'll let you see the ring after dinner.'

Penny smiled over at him. 'Will I need to shield my eyes from the dazzle of the diamonds? Or is it a solitaire like Robin's ring?'

'It's a diamond cluster set in yellow gold.'

'I love solitaires, but as you know, diamond clusters are my favourite.'

Neil did know. He smiled and ate his dinner.

The conversation swung back to the craft fair, and he was happy to talk about that.

'Do you want me to put the kettle on for tea?' Penny offered, standing up before he could stop her, lifting up their plates and taking them over to the sink.

Neil jumped to his feet and relieved her of the plates, placing them down at the side of the sink.

'I'll make the tea. You relax,' he insisted.

Penny smiled and wandered over to breathe in the night air from the garden. 'It's a gorgeous evening. I can sense the autumn.' She took another deep breath.

Neil filled the kettle, but didn't switch it on to boil. Instead, he decided that this was his moment.

The ring box was in his trouser pocket. He turned the twinkle lights on, illuminating the garden.

'Wow! This looks like a fairytale garden,' Penny said, stepping outside and gazing around at the twinkling lights. She looked up at the night sky. 'They're outshining the stars this evening.'

He hoped the diamond ring would outshine everything.

Taking a steadying breath, Neil clasped her hand and gazed at her. He was so tall that she barely came up to his shoulders.

'Someone's in the mood for romance this evening,' Penny said, smiling at him.

'I am,' he said, and then he took the ring box from his pocket and opened it.

The ring glittered under the lights, a floral cluster of seven brilliant–cut diamonds.

Penny gasped when she saw the ring, and realised that Neil was about to propose.

'I love you, Penny. Will you marry me?' Neil's words sounded rich and true in the autumn air, and surrounded by twinkle lights and stars above them, Penny gave Neil her response.

'Yes, I'll marry you, Neil. I love you.'

Neil slipped the ring on her finger.

Penny smiled at him. It was a perfect fit. The cluster of diamonds shone like dazzling starlight as she moved her hand to admire it. The rich, yellow gold enhanced the effect, and she could barely stop looking at it.

'It's the most beautiful ring I've ever seen,' she said, feeling surprised, overwhelmed, almost teary with happiness, but unable to stop smiling.

Neil wrapped her in his arms and kissed her.

Penny melted into his embrace, and felt her world fall into place, here with Neil.

They stood together, wrapped in each other's arms, enjoying the moment.

'I've been planning this for a while,' he said, and started to tell her about keeping his proposal a secret, along with Oliver's secret.

'I'm completely surprised. I never guessed that you were going to do this.' She laughed lightly. 'Everyone is going to be astounded when we announce our engagement.'

'I know it's close to the fair, but it seemed the right time. We can plan a date for the wedding when it suits you.' He was trying to assure her that there was no pressure to set a date, thinking Penny would want a long engagement. It was the first thing he'd got wrong the whole evening.

Penny smiled at him, her eyes alight with excitement. 'When do you think we should get married?'

'I'd marry you tomorrow.' True, impractical, and he knew they couldn't. But it was the truth.

Penny laughed. 'I do have a vintage wedding dress that's made from oyster satin, but maybe that's a bit too fast.'

'Name a date then,' he said, hardly believing that his wishes had come true.

'Autumn is a lovely time of year,' she said. 'So is spring. But I've always wanted to be a snow bride.'

'To get married in the heart of winter? When it's snowing?' He sounded excited at the prospect.

'Yes, it's a fanciful notion, I know, but—'

'Apparently, it snows every winter here in the village.' He gazed at Penny, seeing the excitement in her eyes.

'It doesn't have to be a big, fancy wedding. Just a snowy one.'

Neil nodded. 'Let's do that.'

He kissed her again, and again.

Not only had Penny accepted his proposal, they'd set a time for the wedding.

'Oliver ordered an engagement cake from Bradoch,' he began.

'Yes, Robin showed me pictures of the heart-shaped cake.'

'I ordered mine first.' He explained what had happened.

Penny blinked. 'So, you've got a cake?'

Neil nodded and smiled.

'Where is it?'

'Hidden in the kitchen pantry. And the champagne is chilling in the fridge.'

Penny laughed and wrapped her arms around his neck and kissed him.

Leading her inside, Neil lifted the cake out of the pantry and put it down on the kitchen table.

'A fondant engagement ring!' She sounded delighted.

'Remember that evening up at the castle when someone sent me a picture of a ring?'

Penny nodded.

'Well, it was Bradoch...' Neil told her the whole story, while they took pictures of the cake before cutting two slices.

'I'm keeping this ring forever too,' she said, referring to the icing ring.

Neil's heart felt all the love in the world for Penny, as she confirmed her wish for them to be together forever.

Popping the champagne, they drank a toast to their engagement and their forthcoming wedding, and enjoyed the delicious cake.

'When will we tell Etta, Aileen, Jessy, everyone?' said Penny.

'Now, if you want.'

Penny nodded. She couldn't wait to tell them, and sent a message to Etta and others, knowing the news would circulate fast.

Neil messaged Oliver, Bradoch and Walter with the exciting news.

The surprised but happy responses came back fast.

'Jessy, Muira and most of the other ladies are in the marquee, sorting their stalls,' said Penny. 'She pictured the news sparking around the ladies, catching fire and igniting over to the castle to the laird and Walter.

Neil checked the three messages he'd received, all congratulating him on the news. He confirmed that Bradoch was welcome to put a picture of their engagement cake on the bakery website. Oliver offered to paint a watercolour of Penny's ring, and Neil accepted. Walter cheered!

'Another engagement,' Amy said, sounding astounded when Jessy told her. Amy was in the marquee, but was about to leave and get some sleep.

Sylvia came running over to Jessy. 'Neil proposed to Penny!'

'I know,' said Jessy. 'It's wonderful.'

Jessy and Amy went back for a few minutes to chat to the others.

'Romance is flourishing at the village this year,' said Etta.

'Two engagements.' Kity smiled. 'How romantic.'

Muira, Aileen, Robin, Bee, Elspeth and others were all there, chatting about the news.

'Neil's a goldsmith,' Jessy told Elspeth and Kity. 'So Penny's ring is sure to be beautiful.'

Sylvia squealed with excitement. 'Look! Penny's sent a picture of her ring.'

The others checked their messages and found the picture too.

'A diamond cluster!' said Muira.

'I love my ring,' said Robin, 'but Penny's is gorgeous.'

'They're both beautiful rings,' said Etta.

All the ladies agreed.

As did the men, including Sean, Campbell and Fyn.

'I'm still working at the castle, helping Walter and Gaven,' Jessy said to Amy. 'But you should go and get some sleep.'

Amy nodded. 'It's been a long, busy day.' She gave Jessy a hug, picked up her bags that were empty of her embroidery now that it was displayed on her stall, and headed out into the night.

'Amy,' a man's voice called after her.

She turned to see Knightly running towards her. 'I haven't had a chance to talk to you all day.'

'I saw you earlier, but you were busy with Gaven and Walter,' said Amy. 'I didn't want to interrupt.'

'You should've come over.'

'Well, I'm heading back to the cottage now to get a reasonably early night. But here's the craft bag I promised you. I knocked on your cabin this morning, but you were out.'

Knightly accepted the denim bag. 'Thank you, I'll give it back when the fair is finished.'

Amy smiled, nodded and started to walk away.

'I'll walk you back to the cottage.'

He walked along with her, and they chatted about their preparations for the fair. And about the latest engagement.

'Romance is in the air here,' Amy emphasised. 'As I said before, be warned.'

'Too late,' he admitted, half joking, half true.

Amy laughed, thinking he was only joking.

Tell her, he urged himself, before you miss your chance again. At least see her reaction, when he admitted that he liked her, more than liked her, and wanted to invite her to have dinner with him. A proper dinner date at the castle.

Amy saw a look of turmoil in his eyes. What was he hiding?

Before he could pluck up the nerve to tell her, Jessy's voice rang out behind them through the calm night air.

'Amy!' Jessy hurried to catch up. 'Gaven told me to go and get some sleep. He's dealing with the last minute bookings.'

Amy smiled, pleased that Jessy could get some rest as well.

Knightly closed his heart again, before he'd had a chance to fully open it and express his feelings to Amy. Bad timing? Or fortuitous? Would his revelation ruin their friendship? He never got the chance to decide, because Amy and Jessy bid him goodnight, and hurried away to the cottage.

'See you in the morning at the fair,' Amy called back to him.

Knightly raised his hand in acknowledgment, and walked away to his cabin, wishing he'd told Amy how he felt about her.

The morning of the fair shone bright with a light breeze fluttering through the bunting draped outside the marquees. People had arrived early, hoping to enjoy the whole day of fun events and see all the lovely crafts available at the numerous stalls divided between the two large marquees, and dotted around the front of the castle.

Guests from the castle had breakfast and then headed over to browse the stalls, and everyone from the village was involved in one way or another. It was a popular local event that the community enjoyed annually, and the laird, wearing a classy suit, shirt and tie, was there to welcome everyone.

Knightly wore a white cravat shirt and a bronze brocade waistcoat that had a slight upturn to the collar, creating a classic vintage look. Worn with the cuffs undone, and formal black trousers, anyone expecting to see Knightly the actor would not be disappointed.

Casual didn't suit the occasion, especially when he'd become a highlight with his demonstrations.

The audience in the marquee would be less than those of the hundreds in the theatres, but all his world was a stage, and even though this one was small, his effort was as strong as if he was performing in a popular play.

His kilt and accessories for the Highland Fling were hanging up in his cabin ready for the change of costume in the afternoon. Years of performing on time had instilled a core professionalism in him that was no longer an effort but a habit.

Knightly was prepared to demonstrate his embroidery, and had packed the denim bag Amy had given him. The vintage quality suited his attire, and although he didn't have a stall, Walter had set up a chair and small table on the stage, and he sat there, being entertained himself by the magnificence of the turnout for the fair.

The stage itself had been dressed overnight, and had acquired a curtain rail with a burgundy velvet curtain hanging at one side. Knightly wasn't entirely sure what he was supposed to do — hide behind it if he messed up his fling, or leap out from stage left, kilt swinging? Either way, it presented a theatrical air to the stage.

Walter gave Knightly a thumbs up from across the marquee. Knightly nodded his thanks.

Every effort had clearly been worthwhile. The marquee was abuzz with happy activity.

Knightly assessed the mood of the audience, the crowd. *Cheery.*

He saw Struan striding around in full hotelier mode, providing backup for Gaven, as they toured the stalls checking that everything was okay.

Then Knightly looked across and saw that Amy was busy at her stall, showing customers her embroidery.

Seeming to sense him watching her, Amy looked over at Knightly. Her smile lit up his heart.

She held up a shortbread tin and beckoned to him.

Thinking she'd brought him a tasty treat, Knightly hung his bag on the back of the chair, stepped down from the stage and made his way over to her.

'I brought this for you.' Amy handed him the tin.

'Thank you, I'll indulge later with a cup of tea.'

She laughed. 'Open it.'

He did, and smiled when he saw that the shortbread had been scoffed and replaced with a selection of embroidery thread, crewel wool, and other bits and pieces for his crafting.

'This is even better,' he said. It was true. There was something delightfully enticing about the colourful threads, some with a lovely lustre, others a metallic effect, stranded cotton in autumnal tones, and the soft crewel wool in small skeins that looked too nice to unravel.

Customers tried to engage Amy in conversation, wanting to know about her embroidery patterns and thread.

'I'll see you later, Amy,' Knightly said, and started to head back to the stage to stash his tin. En route, he met Struan in full stride.

Struan stopped, assessed Knightly's attire and smiled. 'I see you're looking the part today.'

'As are you, in your hotel haute couture,' Knightly joked.

Struan laughed. 'Even when we're enjoying ourselves at the fair, we're still in working mode.' Then he looked at the tin. 'Except when it comes to shortbread.'

Knightly opened it and gave Struan a peek.

Struan guffawed. 'Well disguised.'

Knightly tapped the side of his nose, and then they both went on their way.

When he got back to the stage, Knightly noticed that a cup of tea and a buttered soda scone had been left for him on the table. Turning and looking around the crowd, he saw a glimpse of chef's white hat disappear into the sea of stalls.

Sipping his tea and scoffing his scone, Knightly relaxed amid the lively melee in the marquee.

With only crumbs left on his plate, he was approached by two ladies, seemingly fans of his, or so he thought as they appeared to recognise him, calling him by his name.

It was only after he'd been talking to them for five minutes, signing autographs on the craft fair flyer, and waving them off, that he noticed a banner with his name and profession was across the top of the stage.

Walter must've noticed his reaction and smiled over.

Knightly grinned, and then three ladies acquainted with his theatre work, came over to enthuse about his acting.

'We saw you in the theatre in Edinburgh performing in your summer show,' one of them said.

The others nodded, indicating they'd been in the audience.

'Can we have a picture with you?' one of them said.

Happy to oblige, Knightly posed with them, smiling, letting them take several pictures with their phones.

'We're coming back later to see you embroider and dance,' another one of them said.

'I'll see you then,' said Knightly.

And off they went, checking their phones, happy with the pictures.

Showing that he was approachable caused others to come over and talk to Knightly, and the morning flew in, surrounded with chatter and praise for his acting.

And then two ladies came over, smiling, and thrust embroidery hoops at him. White fabric was in the hoops.

'Would you sign your name for us to embroider?' one of them said to him.

Crossed wires were jinxing him lately. Somehow the advertising on the castle's website had given the impression that he'd sign his name for them to embroider in whipped back stitch.

But, ho–hum, he thought, and signed every piece of fabric handed to him with the pencil Amy had given him.

'How do you put your fabric in the hoop?' one lady enquired. 'Do you have a special method to keep it tight?'

Showing them what Amy had shown him, and how to add a piece of backing fabric once the pattern had been drawn on, created a little bit of a crowd around the stage. His demonstration hadn't been scheduled until the afternoon. But he was happy to be part of the fun.

His thread in the shortbread tin got an airing as he showed how he used two strands of the embroidery cotton, and that he used a large eye needle to thread the crewel wool.

Jessy nudged Amy. 'Look at Knightly. His stage is buzzing with people talking to him about his embroidery.'

Amy smiled, seeing him genuinely try to explain the thread, the stitches, and what he'd learned. He pretended to be other characters on stage, but there was no pretence from Knightly at the fair. Just a man with a warm heart trying his best.

'Do you have any pre–cut pieces of white, quilting weight cotton for sale?' A woman said to Aileen, looking at the items on her quilting stall.

Aileen had seen the organised chaos around Knightly, and saw that the woman was holding an empty embroidery hoop that she'd bought from another craft stall.

'Yes,' Aileen lied, and then proceeded to cut pieces of fabric to fit the hoop with plenty to spare around the edges.

Delighted, the customer paid and hurried away, showing others where she'd purchased the pieces of fabric.

Aileen was then inundated with similar requests.

Seeing how busy she was, Fyn came over to help.

This caused even more of a stir.

'That's one of the knitwear models,' a woman whispered to her friend. 'I saw him on the local crafting websites.'

'You're right!' another woman agreed.

This was true. Fyn, Gare and Campbell had recently helped Aileen show her quilts for her website, and modelled Etta and Bee's knitwear that day. The pictures and video of their modelling had been promoted on Aileen, Etta and Bee's websites.

The whispers became louder.

'There's another of them.' A woman pointed at Gare, Fyn's brother. Gare was walking by making a video of the craft fair highlights, becoming one of them in the process.

'And another one, over there beside that woman using the spinning wheel,' someone else shouted, seeing Campbell at Bee's stall.

Campbell became roped into having his photo taken, along with Fyn and Gare.

There was such a flurry of activity, that Gaven came rushing over, thinking there was a stooshie. Then Gaven smiled when he saw knitting patterns being thrust at the three men, and watched them autograph the patterns, and add the ladies' names on request.

'They're all so handsome,' a woman commented.

'And no wonder they say the laird is a local heartthrob,' another lady said unaware he was nearby. 'Have you seen Gaven?'

'Totally gorgeous,' the second woman agreed.

'Thank you,' Gaven said, causing several of them to look round in awe and embarrassment.

Gaven smiled, and went on his way.

When the autograph hunters finally left, Aileen smiled at Fyn. 'I told you that you were modelling material.'

Fyn underplayed his looks. 'I was just happy to help you show your quilts and wear Etta and Bee's knitwear.'

Muira and Sylvia watched from their stall, smiling. They'd closed the sweet shop for the day. Aileen had closed her quilt shop. Others, including Oliver and Fyn had done the same. Bradoch kept his bakery open, but planned to attend the fair on the Sunday.

Sean came over to Muira. 'Campbell's infamous today,' he said jokingly.

'We'll need to keep you in mind for modelling the knitwear,' Muira said to Sean.

'I don't have the looks or the poise,' said Sean, flattered that she'd even suggested this.

'Away ye go,' Muira chided him. 'You'd look gorgeous in one of Etta's Fair Isle jumpers.'

Sean gave Muira a wee peck on the cheek, not wanting to give a big show of affection when she was at the stall.

Muira blushed and smiled.

Sylvia thought about Laurie. He was handsome as well. He'd left the previous night to drive to Edinburgh. She missed him already, and hoped he'd be back in time for the ceilidh.

Amy was demonstrating her thistle embroidery using crewel wool, showing several customers her methods to create the soft effect on the top of the thistle.

Knightly came over to watch Amy, impressed with her skill. It was one thing to have her show him how to stitch the patterns, and another to see her demonstrate what she was capable of.

She glanced up at Knightly, and he tipped his hand, gesturing if she wanted a cup of tea.

Without faltering from her sewing, Amy nodded at Knightly.

He disappeared into the crowd to find chef, or one of the refreshment stalls to grab two cups of tea.

On the way, he saw Elspeth and Kity at their stalls nearby. Customers were watching Elspeth make an owl softie.

'I use a teasel brush on the finished owl to fluff up his feathers,' said Elspeth.

He was learning things all the time.

Kity was knitting a tea cosy, or perhaps it was the makings of a hat. Knightly wasn't sure, but customers were eager to watch Kity knit.

A small crowd were gathered at Bee's stall as she knitted at speed, creating a lace weight shawl. Knightly blinked. She was a fast and accurate knitter. Etta said she was the most skilled knitter in the village, and he could see why.

Etta herself was drawing quite a lot of interest in her cable knitting. Knightly had his eye on a cream Aran knit jumper she had hanging up in her stall. A winter buy, he thought, planning to purchase it later.

Finding tea at a refreshments stall, Knightly headed back to give a cup to Amy, and maybe chat to her. Tell her how much he liked her.

There was no chance of that as he handed her the tea because her stall was even busier when he got back.

Smiling tightly, hiding his disappointment, but pleased that she was doing a roaring trade, he went back to the stage.

Walter intercepted him. 'Remember to give me the nod when you want me to play the music for your dancing.'

'I will,' Knightly assured him, and then checked the time. 'I'd better get back to the cabin and put my kilt on.'

'Aye, the time's fair chomping in,' said Walter.

Robin's textile art stall, and Penny's sewing and mending stall, had extra visitors, as well as customers, wanting to congratulate them on their engagements and see the diamond rings.

Oliver sat at the back of Robin's stall with a sketch pad, drawing ideas he had for his paintings and illustrated picture books. The relief that they were now engaged was evident.

Neil walked by taking tea to Penny, and took a moment to chat to Oliver.

'We're both lucky men,' said Neil.

'We are,' Oliver agreed. 'Did your proposal really go according to plan?' he whispered to Neil.

'It did, but now we're planning our wedding,' said Neil. 'Penny wants to be a snow bride. So a wintertime wedding is on the cards.'

'I'm delighted for you,' said Oliver. 'We haven't set a date yet, but I know we will. And I'll be needing those wedding rings from you.'

Neil nodded, reassuring Oliver he'd make the rings. 'After the fair, I'll start to make our wedding rings.'

'What are you two whispering about now? More secrets?' said Robin.

'No, just discussing my wedding plans,' said Neil. No secrets needed now.

Robin smiled at Neil. 'Penny says she's planning to be a snow bride. What a lovely and romantic idea.'

Knightly was walking by, heading out, and overheard the happy chatter about the engagements and wedding plans, wishing he was in a similar position with Amy. That's when it struck him deeply. He was truly thinking of Amy like this. More than a sweet romance. Something inside him sparked, spurring him to make a bold move. Just not what Amy was expecting, or anyone else in the community.

Before he could make any decisions, he needed to gather information, find out if his plan was feasible, practical, and determine if Amy had romantic feelings for him.

This would take time. But Amy was leaving on the Monday morning. That was that. He had to figure things out now.

CHAPTER SIXTEEN

Wearing a white ghillie shirt with his kilt and sporran, knee–length socks with flashes tucked into the tops, and his Highland dancing shoes that he'd kept from his stage performance, Knightly went back into the marquee.

As he headed towards the stage, he walked by Amy and Jessy at a stall. They didn't see him, and were so intent on admiring a vintage wooden sewing box on legs, like an occasional table. The cantilever style enabled it to be opened on three levels with lots of dookits to store thread and other items. The stallholder was serving another customer.

Knightly overheard Amy. 'I love sewing boxes like this. But it's so expensive.'

Jessy agreed, and they moved on to go back to Amy's stall.

Knightly called to Jessy. 'Could I have a word about...the stage, Jessy?'

'Yes,' Jessy said, smiling and wondering how she could help.

Amy walked back to her stall.

'I need you to do me a favour,' Knightly whispered hurriedly.

Jessy nodded.

'I'd like you to buy that sewing box Amy was looking at for me. Bill me, and have it sent to my cabin.' He winked.

Jessy smiled, happy to be part of the conspiratorial surprise for Amy. 'I'll do that.'

'I don't want Amy to know.'

Jessy nodded. 'I know hee–haw.'

Leaving Jessy to purchase the gift for Amy, Knightly headed to the stage. Walter was lifting the table and chair aside. 'Just in case you go haywire.'

Although Knightly was due to do the Highland Fling, which was danced on the one spot, he was pleased that nothing was nearby.

'Cheers, Walter.'

By now, Knightly's kilt had attracted people's attention, and they started to come over to the stage to see his performance.

Gare came over to the stage, holding a video camera. 'I'm filming you dancing,' he informed him.

Knightly nodded. 'Yes, I agreed this with Gaven.'

'Aye, but I wanted to reassure you that if your kilt flies up and your dangleberries are on show, I'll edit them out of the video before it goes up on the castle's website.'

'Good to know. But I'm not going commando.'

'No worries then,' said Gare, adjusting the video camera and standing back where he could capture the full performance.

Amy had a clear view of the stage, and smiled at Knightly.

His heart reacted seeing her. He needed to dance this well and not make a complete mess of it.

Knightly saw Walter and gave him the thumbs up, expecting the opening notes of the music to ring out in the marquee. Instead, Walter turned two spotlights on, highlighting Knightly in the bright glow.

Yes, Knightly thought, standing in the glare, as he'd done before on stage, seeing the eager faces watching him, no hiding any messy steps today.

As the music began, Knightly started dancing, jumping, turning and twirling. His kilt and sporran swung in time to the music, and the energetic dance moves came back to him without faltering. The seasoned performer in him danced it as if he was on stage in a theatre.

The audience in the marquee cheered and applauded when he finished dancing.

Knightly took a bow, and then stepped behind the curtain.

When he emerged again, Gaven and Struan were standing in front of the stage applauding along with the crowd.

Knightly smiled at Amy.

She smiled at him and clapped, nodding, assuring him of his performance.

And beside her was Jessy, giving Knightly a slightly different nod, indicating that the sewing box had been secured.

The first day of the craft fair was a resounding success. People had turned up from other towns, as well as further afield, including Edinburgh. The news on the Mullcairn show, and in the papers, had brought lots of people to the fair. The local bed and breakfast accommodation was fully booked.

Some people were now heading home, while those staying at the castle planned to have dinner and enjoy the whole craft fair weekend.

'Come and join us for dinner,' Gaven said to Knightly, including Struan in his plans.

'I'll pop to the cabin and get changed,' said Knightly, taking them up on their offer.

Looking around, he wondered where Amy had gone.

Jessy hurried over to Knightly. 'The sewing box will be delivered to your cabin in a wee while.'

'Where's Amy?'

'I encouraged her to go back to my cottage and relax,' said Jessy. 'It'll be another hectic day tomorrow, and the ceilidh party at night.'

Knightly forced a smile. 'That was a sensible suggestion.' Though he wished he'd had a chance to talk to her before she'd left the marquee.

Jessy walked away to assist Walter, leaving Knightly standing on his own.

He watched Robin and Oliver wrapped in each other's arms, and likewise, Neil and Penny. Although happy for them, he was nonetheless feeling the longing to have a loving relationship, a lasting romance.

Knightly could see the romances, like sparks, igniting between other couples in the community. Aileen and Fyn. Muira and Sean. Bee and Campbell. He stopped and shook away the thoughts that he had no one special. But maybe he could have, if he handled things properly with Amy. Or was this just a dream that was never going to work?

Heading out of the marquee, Knightly walked to his cabin, got changed into his previous outfit, and went back to the castle to join the laird and others for dinner.

Amy had sold numerous items of her embroidery, kits, patterns and thread. It had been a successful sales day. And she'd enjoyed demonstrating her embroidery, while meeting people and showing them how she created her designs.

But she did feel tired. Not from the long day at the fair, but from the emotional effect Knightly had on her. It was hard to deny the attraction between them, and even harder the more she got to know him, and see that he was kind, talented, fun to be with, willing to risk making a fool of himself, then showing how accomplished he could be.

'Don't overstuff your knitted robin,' Elspeth advised Sylvia, showing her how she made the softie.

Sylvia watched Elspeth demonstrate her technique, on the second day of the fair, having missed it the previous day.

'I've got the pattern, and the yarn,' said Sylvia. 'But it's handy to see how you stitch the robin together.'

Other people were watching Elspeth make the robin, and several interested faces peered at her sitting at her stall.

'I'm using scraps of yarn to stuff the robin,' Elspeth explained.

'That's a great idea,' said Sylvia.

'And I use yarn to sew the seams and stitch on the eyes and beak,' Elspeth added.

Elspeth had demonstrated how she knitted socks, and this was another project of interest at her stall.

Customers had bought up most of the yarn Elspeth had brought with her from the island, making the trip a success for business, while having fun at the fair and meeting up with the crafting bee ladies.

Kity felt the same. Her knitting stall was emptying as the second day wore on, and she'd enjoyed staying at Etta's cottage. She'd demonstrated knitting a beautiful brioche scarf and an intarsia scarf showing her colourwork skills. The patterns were on her website, along with the yarn to knit them. But lots of customers had bought these from Kity's stall.

Amy showed customers how she embroidered her bee garden pattern, satin stitching the petals on the cornflowers, daisies, foxgloves and sunflowers, and adding French knots, colonial knots, stem stitches and back stitches.

Bee's lace weight knitting skills were appreciated by onlookers, and many people tried their hand at spinning their own yarn using the small drop spindles.

Aileen demonstrated English paper piecing methods to make a quilt. She showed how she made hexies, and sold all her pre–cut bundles of fabric.

The excitement was still circulating about the two new engagements, and Penny and Robin's stalls were key attractions at the fair. People liked seeing Penny's sewing and mending methods to repair items of clothing. And Robin's textile art paintings sold out. Oliver and Neil were there again to help when needed.

Bradoch had closed his bakery and ventured up to the fair, intending to wander around and see all the stalls, and relax. But his plans went awry when he was roped into helping chef cater for the extra guests at the castle.

The second day of the craft fair was busier than the first. Gaven circulated around the main marquee, talking to visitors and stallholders, and chatted to Knightly beside the stage. Struan and Walter were there too, ensuring the event ran according to plan.

'The fair has been a huge success,' Gaven said to Knightly. 'Thanks for being part of it.'

'I've enjoyed the friendship and fun,' said Knightly.

Wearing his kilt, ready for his final dance performance, Knightly glanced around at the busy stalls. His embroidery hoops were on the table, and he'd been showing people his crewel work bumblebee, and had finished satin stitching most of his acorn pattern.

Knightly noticed a figure walk into the marquee. 'Mullcairn is here.'

Gaven looked over, and there was the radio presenter, dressed in a Fair Isle jumper, shirt and smart trousers, glancing around the stalls.

'Let's go over and welcome him,' said Gaven, encouraging Knightly to go with him.

The two of them made a beeline for Mullcairn.

'Knightly!' Mullcairn said, pleased to see him.

'This is Gaven,' said Knightly.

Mullcairn smiled warmly and shook hands with the laird.

'Delighted you could come along to our fair,' said Gaven. 'Can I get you a refreshment? Or would you prefer to have a look around first?'

'I'd love a nosy at the stalls,' said Mullcairn. 'And I'm keeping a lookout for Etta. Is she here?'

'Yes, she's over beside Amy and a few of the other ladies.' Knightly gestured in the direction of Etta's stall.

'Lead the way,' Mullcairn said, bolstering himself to meet Etta.

Having seen Mullcairn arrive, Walter ran over to Etta's stall where she was sitting knitting a jumper. Her cable demonstrations had been popular, and she'd sold almost all of her jumpers and other knitted garments. She wore a ditsy print skirt in shades of blue and neutral tones, a white blouse, and a light blue cardigan she'd knitted. Her silvery blonde hair was neatly styled.

'Etta!' Walter shouted to her. 'Mullcairn is in the marquee!'

Etta stopped knitting, feeling a rush of excitement. She glanced around, not knowing what direction her heartthrob was coming from. For a moment, she didn't think she could meet him without blushing. 'I think I'll make a run for it,' she said to Walter, sounding panicky.

'You can run, Etta, but I'll catch you,' Mullcairn said, approaching her from behind.

Etta glanced round and there he was, a strong, fine looking man, taller than she'd imagined, and with a warm smile showing how pleased he was to see her.

'Mullcairn!' Etta gasped. 'You're here!' She blinked, taking in the Fair Isle jumper he was wearing. 'That's the jumper I knitted for you.'

Mullcairn puffed up his chest and let her have a proper look at him wearing it. 'I love it. Comfy, classy. I love a Fair Isle jumper.' Then he opened his arms wide. 'Are you not going to give me a welcome, Etta?'

Etta's heart jumped with joy, and without any hesitation she gave Mullcairn a hug, feeling him wrap his arms around her.

'That's more like it,' said Mullcairn. Then he smiled right at her. 'You're looking lovely, Etta.'

There was no hiding her blushes, and it was clear that Mullcairn did like her.

'Okay, let me see what you've got on your stall,' said Mullcairn.

'There's not much left,' Etta told him. 'The fair has been jumping all weekend.'

'In that case, can I persuade you to give me a tour of the other stalls?' Mullcairn looked around. 'Where's Muira, Sylvia, Jessy and Aileen?'

Hearing their names, they all waved to him from their stalls nearby. Tucked into a niche, Mullcairn let Etta give him a tour of the stalls and introduced him to all the ladies.

Then the lights dimmed, the music sounded, and Knightly started to dance the Highland Fling.

Etta took Mullcairn over to watch the actor's last performance of the fair.

Mullcairn joined in the clapping towards the end of the dance, along with others in the audience at the front of the stage.

Knightly finished and took a bow, smiling.

Amy was there again, watching Knightly, feeling a slight ache in her heart, knowing the weekend was coming to a close.

But the ceilidh party beckoned, and a night of dancing and romancing at the castle.

A live band played in a corner of the function room, and buffet tables were set up on one side.

Couples were already up dancing when Amy arrived. Jessy was on duty, but she was dressed to join in the ceilidh.

All the women wore dresses or skirts and blouses, of various styles, with many adding a touch of tartan. Amy's sapphire blue dress had a slightly flared skirt and, like most of the ladies, she'd wore low heel shoes she could dance in.

She looked around and saw Robin and Oliver wrapped in each other's arms, dancing. Oliver wore a dark shirt and dark waistcoat with his kilt, and Robin's midnight blue dress glittered with sparkles. Nearby, Penny and Neil were deep in loving conversation. Penny's vintage tea dress suited her, and Neil wore a kilt, shirt and waistcoat.

Laurie had arrived as promised and was dancing with Sylvia.

Mullcairn was there, wearing a traditional kilt and white shirt, and Amy watched him clasp Etta's hand and lead her smiling on to the dance floor. Etta wore the dress she'd bought from Penny. Amy thought Mullcairn and Etta looked happy together enjoying the ceilidh.

Muira was there with Sean, along with Campbell and Bee. They were all chatting together near the buffet.

Fyn arrived with Aileen, both looking excited to be there, and eager to join in the dancing.

Elspeth was dancing with Gaven, though there was nothing but friendship between them. The laird was the epitome of kilted class and a skilled dancer.

Struan had asked Kity to dance with him, and again, only in polite social friendship.

The castle's guests were there, and as Amy continued to glance around the lively function room, she wondered where Knightly was.

Knightly breathed in the fresh, night air as he strode towards the castle from his cabin.

Wearing his lace–up ghillie shirt, kilt and sporran, he had an unintentional swagger to him.

After the long day at the fair, he'd gone back to his cabin to shower and get changed for the ceilidh. His dark hair was ruffled, as if indicating his inner turmoil.

He ran a hand through his unruly hair that he hadn't bothered trying to tame after showering. Time was wearing on, and now...it was the ceilidh night, and Amy was due to leave the next morning.

The thought of this tied his stomach in knots. Despite putting on a cheery face during the day in the marquee, his heart ached at the prospect of Amy leaving. His acting skills surely saved the day. No one guessed that his relaxed manner hid a troubled heart.

Part of him told himself to be bold. Tell her how he felt, and let the chips fall where they wanted. But was that wise? He wasn't even sure how Amy felt about him.

Knightly was still arguing with himself as he saw the castle, the windows all lit up, the entrance aglow with a warm welcome, and lively music pouring out into the night air. The castle lived up to its reputation for putting on wonderful ceilidh parties, and he hoped that Amy was there so he could dance with her.

Sweeping his hair back, and bucking up, Knightly made a stylish entrance, striding into the function room, and causing a few guests to glance, acknowledging his arrival.

Amy was standing at the buffet and saw Knightly scan the room. Was he looking for her? She sensed he was.

Her gaze seemed to draw his attention, and his heart reacted when he saw her.

Striding over, full swagger, unintentional or not, he cut a fine figure as he approached her.

Her heart reacted to him too, and that feeling she'd had all day, of missing him even though he'd been there in the marquee, increased when she saw him.

'You look lovely this evening, Amy.'

That rich voice of his resonated through her, and she longed for him to take her in his arms and tell her that everything would work out fine. But she knew this was a silly notion. How could it when she was leaving, and their lives were due to continue in the separate worlds they'd come from? There was no way to resolve this, she chided herself. Maybe that's just how it was always meant to be with her and Knightly. Like one of his plays, the story was due to come to an end after the last dance of the evening. Curtain down. And everyone would go home, including her, back to the town where she'd left her life on ice.

She smiled at Knightly, hoping none of her wayward thoughts had revealed themselves to him.

He glanced at the buffet. 'Have you had anything to eat yet?'

'No, I was about to. Everything looks so delicious.'

'We're spoiled for choice. Though those vol–au–vents look tasty. I'm not sure what's in them.'

'Haggis,' said Walter, overhearing him as he hurried by. 'Delicious. Grab one while they're going.'

'I will, Walter.' Knightly lifted one of the light pastry cases filled with haggis and took a bite. And then nodded at Amy.

Amy decided to try one. 'Mmmm.' She nodded too. And then they laughed, trying to catch the flakes of pastry on to plates.

'Hogging all the tasty bites, eh?' Mullcairn said, approaching them with Etta at his side. 'You two should be up dancing and romancing.'

Knightly spluttered. No subtle hints from Mullcairn. Though maybe that's what was needed, he thought.

'You're right,' Knightly said to Mullcairn. He put his plate down and then turned to Amy. 'Would you care to dance?'

'I would,' she said, smiling, putting her plate aside.

Knightly clasped her hand and led her into a lively dance, and soon they were twirling and burling around, enjoying themselves.

The sound of the live band playing popular songs along with traditional Scottish dance music, filled the room for the remainder of the night.

There was no lull in the dancing, as one number merged into the next, and those inclined to dance their socks off, could join in a jig and then into a reel.

Amy felt happily exhausted.

'Shall we sit the next one out?' Knightly called to her as they linked arms and burled around.

'Yes,' she said, laughing.

Clasping her hand, Knightly led Amy away from the dancing over to the buffet.

She felt his strong, elegant fingers wrap around hers, and unless she was mistaken, he didn't want to let go. She didn't want him to either, and so there they were, deciding what to eat and drink at the buffet, holding hands, as if they were both trying to hold on to the evening as the night wore on.

The buffet was extensive. Plates were piled with traditional Scottish fare, along with chef's selection of other dishes to tempt them, including favourites such as mashed tattie and cheddar pies, terrines of neeps and tatties, mini quiche, sausage rolls and salads. Cakes galore included Dundee cake and Victoria sponge filled with buttercream and raspberry jam. There was strawberry trifle and shortbread. And plenty to drink, from whisky cocktails to cups of tea.

Mullcairn stood at the side of the buffet, talking into his phone, recording snippets for his forthcoming radio show.

'I'm here at the laird's magnificent castle, kilted and joining in the ceilidh dancing. The autumn craft fair was a huge success, and I met lots of local residents, including Etta. She's here with me now. Say hello to the listeners, Etta.'

'Hello. Mullcairn's a rascal. He's been dancing me around the floor all night.'

'There you go,' said Mullcairn. 'We're having a grand time at the castle's ceilidh. I'm fair chuffed.'

Knightly laughed, overhearing him.

'And to my right is another rascal, the actor, Knightly,' Mullcairn announced into his phone, keeping the recording going. 'He embroidered his acorns, a bumble, and danced a lively Highland Fling. Now he's munching all the tasty stuff at the buffet, and dancing with Amy.'

Amy giggled.

'Folk loved your Highland dancing, Knightly,' said Mullcairn. 'Did you enjoy yourself?'

'I did,' said Knightly. 'Though a couple of times I nearly whirled off the stage.'

Mullcairn pretended to sound frightened at the thought of this. 'Oh, scary biscuits!'

Gaven went by and Mullcairn called out to him. 'Gaven, can you say a wee word to the listeners?'

Gaven stepped close and spoke into Mullcairn's phone. 'The autumn fair this year was busier than ever. And we're planning other events at the castle for the winter and Christmas.'

'I have a lovely room in the castle with a great view of the loch,' Mullcairn added. 'I'm keen to come back here to enjoy your festive parties.'

'You'll be made welcome,' Gaven assured him.

'Okay, folks,' Mullcairn concluded. 'I'm away to skirl Etta around the floor. So, I suppose it'll be time for a wee jingle and then on with the show.'

Mullcairn clicked his phone off and smiled at Etta. 'This will air as part of my next show on the radio. If you're ever up in Edinburgh, pop into the studio. I'll give you a tour.'

Etta was tempted to accept Mullcairn's invitation. 'Maybe I will.'

Mullcairn smiled at her. 'Come on, let's join in the dancing.' Clasping her hand, he led her into another lively reel.

Knightly lifted two cups of tea and handed one to Amy.

'Cheers,' he said.

Amy tipped her cup against his. 'Cheers.'

They chatted while sipping their tea.

'What time are you leaving in the morning?' he said.

'Early. I've packed my car ready to go.'

He felt a dagger cut through his heart. 'Will you have time for breakfast with me before you leave?'

'I'm leaving at the crack of dawn.'

He nodded. 'I bought something for you. A wee gift, as a thank you for teaching me embroidery and for putting up with my nonsense.'

'You're not so bad,' she teased him. 'Though you didn't need to buy me anything.'

He took out his phone and showed her a picture of what he'd bought.

'The sewing box!' she exclaimed. 'That's too much, but thank you. I suppose I have something extra to pack in my car.'

Knightly shook his head. 'No, I'll deliver it to you. Special delivery to your home in the town.'

Amy went to object, thinking it was unnecessary to post it off to her. 'I could take it with me.'

'I was thinking that I could deliver it to you myself.' His deep voice sounded tentative, hoping she'd agree for him to come and visit her.

Amy blinked, taken aback by his offer. 'You'll come to my town?'

He stepped closer. 'If that's okay with you.'

'It is.'

Knightly stepped closer still, wrapping his arms around her gently and gazing down at her. 'I've been wanting to ask if you'd like to have dinner with me.'

'Like a dinner date?' she said hopefully.

Knightly nodded. 'Yes.'

'I'd like that.'

He pulled her closer, feeling as if they did have a chance at happiness together.

'I have to tell you that I've been falling in love with you since I met you.'

Amy gasped, hearing him say what she longed to hear. 'I've felt the same.'

'I know our worlds are apart right now, but I've been having a look at properties for lease in your town,' he revealed. 'And it's a lot closer to Edinburgh than the village. As I've been wanting to live outwith the city, this village is lovely, but your small town looks idyllic. I could travel up to Edinburgh for my shows, but I don't work all the time. So you'd have to put up with me being around a lot more.'

'I think I could do that,' she said playfully.

'Amethyst and the actor.' His rich voice sounded out the words. 'I believe this could work, and we could enjoy the future together. You and me, Amy.'

Waves of emotion, excitement, love for this wonderful man, swirled around her, and in the midst of it she said... 'Yes, I believe we could.'

Knightly leaned down and kissed her.

Amy didn't resist, and kissed him, feeling the sparks of attraction burst into romantic fire.

For the remainder of the ceilidh, everyone, including Knightly and Amy, joined in the dancing, agreeing that this was the most successful and happiest fair they'd ever had at the castle.

Later, Knightly walked Amy back to the cottage. They walked hand in hand together.

The night air was heady with the scent of the greenery and the trees arching over the path from the castle to the cottage.

'It's lovely here,' said Amy. 'I should've visited Jessy before this. But when my parents left the town two years ago, I threw myself wholeheartedly into building up my business.'

'I've been talking to Jessy, and she says she likes going to visit you in the town. She told me what a nice town it is, and how hard you've worked to establish your business there.'

They walked on, and then Knightly saw the path lead off into the trees.

'Are you up for one more night–time adventure?' he said.

Amy smiled and nodded.

They ventured along to the clearing in the trees they'd been to before, and stood there surrounded by all the little twinkle lights.

Amy gazed around her. 'It really does look like a fairytale.'

Knightly felt his heart fill with love for Amy, and gently pulled her close. 'We can make our own fairytale wherever we are, as long as we're together.'

'I think you'll love my wee town,' she said.

Knightly nodded. He was sure of this, and of the love they had for each other.

Leaning down he kissed her, again and again, in the heart of the fairytale surroundings, assured of their own happy ever after.

End

About the Author:

De-ann Black is a bestselling author, scriptwriter and former newspaper journalist. She has over 100 books published. Romance, thrillers, espionage novels, action adventure. And children's books (non-fiction rocket science books and children's fiction). She became an Amazon All-Star author in 2014 and 2015.

She previously worked as a full-time newspaper journalist for several years. She had her own weekly columns in the press. This included being a motoring correspondent where she got to test drive cars every week for the press for three years.

Before being asked to work for the press, De-ann worked in magazine editorial writing everything from fashion features to social news. She was the marketing editor of a glossy magazine.

She is also a professional artist and illustrator. Embroidery design, fabric design, dressmaking, sewing, knitting and fashion are part of her work.

Additionally, De-ann has always been interested in fitness, and was a fitness and bodybuilding champion, 100 metre runner and mountaineer. As a former N.A.B.B.A. Miss Scotland, she had a weekly fitness show on the radio that ran for over three years.

De-ann trained in Shukokai karate, boxing, kickboxing, Dayan Qigong and Jiu Jitsu. She is currently based in Scotland.

Her 16 colouring books are available in paperback, including her latest Summer Nature Colouring Book and Flower Nature Colouring Book.

Her latest embroidery pattern books include: Floral Garden Embroidery Patterns, Christmas & Winter Embroidery Patterns, Floral Spring Embroidery Patterns and Sea Theme Embroidery Patterns.

Website: Find out more at: www.de-annblack.com

Fabric, Wallpaper & Home Decor Collections:
De-ann's fabric designs and wallpaper collections, and home decor items, including her popular Scottish Garden Thistles patterns, are available from Spoonflower.
www.de-annblack.com/spoonflower

Also by De-ann Black (Romance, Action/Thrillers & Children's books). See her Amazon Author page or website for further details about her books, screenplays, illustrations, art, fabric designs and embroidery patterns.

Amazon Author page:
www.De-annBlack.com/Amazon

Romance books:

Scottish Loch Romance series:
1. Sewing & Mending Cottage
2. Scottish Loch Summer Romance
3. Sweet Music
4. Knitting Bee
5. Autumn Romance

Music, Dance & Romance series:
1. The Sweetest Waltz
2. Knitting & Starlight

Snow Bells Haven series:
1. Snow Bells Christmas
2. Snow Bells Wedding
3. Love & Lyrics

Scottish Highlands & Island Romance series:
1. Scottish Island Knitting Bee
2. Scottish Island Fairytale Castle
3. Vintage Dress Shop on the Island
4. Fairytale Christmas on the Island

Quilting Bee & Tea Shop series:
1. The Quilting Bee
2. The Tea Shop by the Sea
3. Embroidery Cottage
4. Knitting Shop by the Sea
5. Christmas Weddings

The Cure for Love Romance series:
1. The Cure for Love
2. The Cure for Love at Christmas

Sewing, Crafts & Quilting series:
1. The Sewing Bee
2. The Sewing Shop
3. Knitting Cottage (Scottish Highland romance)
4. Scottish Highlands Christmas Wedding

Cottages, Cakes & Crafts series:
1. The Flower Hunter's Cottage
2. The Sewing Bee by the Sea
3. The Beemaster's Cottage
4. The Chocolatier's Cottage
5. The Bookshop by the Seaside
6. The Dressmaker's Cottage

Scottish Chateau, Colouring & Crafts series:
1. Christmas Cake Chateau
2. Colouring Book Cottage

Summer Sewing Bee

Sewing, Knitting & Baking series:
1. The Tea Shop
2. The Sewing Bee & Afternoon Tea
3. The Christmas Knitting Bee
4. Champagne Chic Lemonade Money
5. The Vintage Sewing & Knitting Bee

Tea Dress Shop series:
1. The Tea Dress Shop At Christmas
2. The Fairytale Tea Dress Shop In Edinburgh
3. The Vintage Tea Dress Shop In Summer

The Tea Shop & Tearoom series:
1. The Christmas Tea Shop & Bakery
2. The Christmas Chocolatier
3. The Chocolate Cake Shop in New York at Christmas
4. The Bakery by the Seaside
5. Shed in the City

Christmas Romance series:
1. Christmas Romance in Paris
2. Christmas Romance in Scotland

Oops! I'm the Paparazzi series:
1. Oops! I'm the Paparazzi
2. Oops! I'm Up To Mischief
3. Oops! I'm the Paparazzi, Again

The Bitch-Proof Suit series:
1. The Bitch-Proof Suit
2. The Bitch-Proof Romance
3. The Bitch-Proof Bride
4. The Bitch-Proof Wedding

Heather Park: Regency Romance
Dublin Girl
Why Are All The Good Guys Total Monsters?
I'm Holding Out For A Vampire Boyfriend

Action/Thriller books:
Knight in Miami
Agency Agenda
Love Him Forever
Someone Worse
Electric Shadows
The Strife Of Riley
Shadows Of Murder
Cast a Dark Shadow

Children's books:
Faeriefied
Secondhand Spooks
Poison-Wynd
Wormhole Wynd
Science Fashion
School For Aliens

Colouring books:
Summer Nature
Flower Nature
Summer Garden
Spring Garden
Autumn Garden
Sea Dream
Festive Christmas
Christmas Garden
Christmas Theme
Flower Bee
Wild Garden
Faerie Garden Spring
Flower Hunter
Stargazer Space
Bee Garden
Scottish Garden
Seasons

Embroidery Design books:
Sea Theme Embroidery Patterns
Floral Garden Embroidery Patterns
Christmas & Winter Embroidery Patterns
Floral Spring Embroidery Patterns
Floral Nature Embroidery Designs
Scottish Garden Embroidery Designs

Printed in Great Britain
by Amazon